## DEADLY GIFT

Harry Bronson seemed an ordinary enough young man, an inventive engineer with a healthy interest in things young men generally are interested in and a hearty contempt for the claptrap of ESP. But there were oddities about him, too. He remembered not a single thing of his life before the age of ten, for one. For another, he was loaded for bear with ESP talent.

# PSTALEMATE
# LESTER
# DEL REY

A BERKLEY MEDALLION BOOK
PUBLISHED BY
BERKLEY PUBLISHING CORPORATION

*This was to be dedicated to
Judy-Lynn Benjamin,
a most welcome Primate.*

*Now, happily it is to
JUDY-LYNN DEL REY,
a most charming wife!*

# CONTENTS

# I.

# HELL

Martha woke to the muted sound of steps outside her door. In the brief moment before she heard the cover of the spyhole being slipped back, she slitted her eyes enough to scan the illusion of the room.

It was still there, small but comfortable, imitating a private room in an expensive sanatorium. A sturdy door faced a thick-paned window, now showing night outside. Soft light fell on the subdued cheerfulness of draperies, rugs, a padded chair, a quilted table under a mirror that was set into the wall, and a bed that almost hid its hospital functionalism. There was even an image of her, counterfeited into the mirror—a stout figure in flowered pajamas and robe, lying with pulled-up knees, staring back with slitted eyes. Year after year, the evil ones had aged the image until the hair over the slack-sullen face was almost completely gray. Had she been weak enough to live, she might have looked something like that by now.

The creatures were subtly thorough—and always too quick for her. In twenty of the Boy's years, she had never caught them before the room and the image were complete.

She heard the spyhole cover move and closed her eyes before the alien thing could see her. From the heavy breathing, she knew it was wearing the MacAndrews this time. Then the door opened, and she heard heavy steps moving—

*Henry!*

—reproving asthmatic voice with its wheezing kindness and worry she had expected from the MacAndrews. "Well, Martha, what's all this the nurse tells me about your not eating again? We can't have that, you know. You don't want us to go back to forced feeding now, do you?"

The voice halted, waiting for an answer, but she couldn't be tricked into an argument that easily. In spite of all their wiles, she had accepted her apparent control of her body as only more illusion, and she was tired of their attempts to prove that she wasn't dead—to break down her resistance—to reach that part of her which held her firmly locked between here and the tunnel to the world.

She drew back down the slippery ramp in her mind, back near the deep well that went blackly down and down. Once that had frightened her; it would have been so easy to slip and go spinning into the depths, never to land, plummeting forever deeper into the blackness of herself while they took over where she had been. But now she was used to it, and she retreated until she could barely hear the murmur of the MacAndrews voice, still cajoling her. He was being silly. She wouldn't eat the food with the drugs to make her confess any more than she would ever believe all the lies they spread around her. She knew she was dead, and she knew where she was, just as she knew that eventually she must go where they wanted. But not yet—not before she could complete her duty to the Boy!

In the end, of course, she must be damned for the thing she had done to herself. Perhaps these were only lesser creatures, trying to do their proper work on her. But they couldn't send her on until they could prove she had done it to herself or trick her into admitting it. So far they'd failed. She'd been too clever for them; she'd made what happened to her seem like an accident, she'd seen through their illusions, and she would never confess. She couldn't go with them or down into the depths of herself while the Boy was still there, thick with her taint—

*Henry!*

10

—faint sound of the MacAndrews sighing. She crept back from the black well and waited, listening to the scuff of the carpet, the click of the door, and the final sound of the steps down the hall, before the MacAndrews could change back into what it really was. She had won again.

She was sure that they'd turned off the room, but she was too tired to look, knowing it was useless. It was better this way, in the damp blackness around her, where she could lie curled hair so pretty roses in the vase for ashes to ashes all over her head like a cloud of doom for the slightest sin in the back seat of judgment . . .

She caught herself, grabbing frantically for the slithery walls that were already dropping to the bottomless pit. She clawed and fought, until she found the ladder of the old verse—the one she'd had revealed to her after the Change. She felt a skittering memory of alienness and things ran ahead of her awareness, but then she had begun the words of the poem that summed her needs, and she was reciting it over and over, climbing back toward the stability between the pit and the illusion beyond her:

> Mating hating, waiting sating,
>    Slip to sleep in sleuthy slumber;
> Humble fumble, mumble jumble—
>    Kill the cub that cawls encumber.

Sometimes now she could no longer understand it all, but it still served. Distilled from her frantically escaped mind, the words still drew her back, let her relax to something that would be almost sleep in the living. She could no longer find the way out when her mind was tense. Once the whole world was open at all times, but now there was only the single tunnel to the Boy, and she could not reach that until everything else was blanked from her mind and she could draw help from the symbol she had planted. Such a tiny opening toward him—

*Henry!*

—grim, desperate urgency in her need to get back. But at last the murky thread appeared, and she could will her way into the tunnel it marked. She moved outward through

11

infinities of distance, swimming toward the once-familiar goal. Slowly, a richness and width appeared in the tunnel. Then well-known pathways and perception scenery, a parting to let her in. For a second, the familiarity soothed her, until the horror of the developing patterns of what might be, must be, struck her again. Here, still, she could catch the faint wisps of what was to come, though the tainted power no longer operated through either her will or the awareness around her.

The patterns of dark possession were shaping there—patterns that must not be. There was the Man in White, a dim figure from before, just dawning again on the pattern of the Boy. She'd thought the Man in White was erased long before, but he wouldn't rest. Lately, his shadow had come back, to meddle and to ruin, as he'd done to her plans for the Boy when she had first meant the Love Death. Evil was to be let in again—evil that the Man in White himself had sealed out with unknowingness! And there was the Grim Man, with his yearning and his unclean desires for an evil that should not be his, bringing with him something . . .

She strained in the closed area, and for a brief moment her mind seemed to clear and she could see. It was the Girl—the Tainted Girl! Taint to take the Boy from her, to warp him to the Man in White, to lead him to horror!

Martha wanted to cry for the forlornness of the Girl, but she had only tears enough for her own impotency. Even now, the veils were closing on her, too strong for the force of her own dead mind. They were like dust to foretell the wind, and she could do nothing directly. Was all her love for the Boy to come to nothing, all her willing of his death at the cost of her own sure damnation to be denied? There must be some impossible way to reach him, to shelter him from what was inevitable somehow, to prevent foretold and certain evil again. But she was so tired, so weak, and the thing that they had grown in her brain was hurting again—

*Henry!*

—pain!

12

## II.

## STAIRS

As he drove the modified Citroën up Washington Street, Harry Bronson was aware that he was a fool for even thinking of stopping in at the Primates instead of heading directly home. No sensible man should be out at all on such a night, when the unseasonably late and heavy snowfall had already turned from slush to ice on the streets, making Manhattan a disaster area for everything that moved.

Ordinarily, Harry was anything but an outdoor man, even in good weather, though his natural wiriness and effortless coordination often fooled the sports cultists into making unwelcome overtures. His skin seemed well pigmented, but it burned horribly in the summer sun. His eyes were overly sensitive, adjusted for a lower-than-normal light level. His brown hair was baby fine, falling in a tangle across his face at the whim of the faintest breeze. Finally, his nose had been broken in a high school rocket experiment and now ached and developed sniffles at the first touch of cold air. Generally, he regarded the rigors of nature with as little favor as he did any needless athletics or things like parlor guessing games.

But the storm had come up unexpectedly to refute all weather predictions. He'd listened to the early reports, then decided he couldn't wait longer to locate the duplicates of the engineering reports his partner, Sid Greenwald, had carelessly left behind. Sid's house was forty miles out in New Jersey, but that should have been less than an hour's drive each way. Besides, Harry rather wanted to give the car a decent test in snow again, now that he'd retuned his engine.

He hadn't counted on the pileup of flashy, overpowered, and undertractioned Detroit cars at the turnpike exit or the stupidity of the average driver on icing roads. He'd been held up for nearly two hours while cars were slowly pulled off the icy ramp ahead of him. Then he'd decided against the parkway, where traffic would also be thick, and had somehow managed to get lost on the back roads. By the time he reached Sid's house and managed to locate the papers in Sid's files, it was already fully dark outside. He'd debated staying the night but had given up the idea when he found nothing left that was fit to eat. Mercifully, the roads were almost free of traffic on the way back, but it was nearly eleven before he finally wheeled through the Holland Tunnel.

A light ahead of him turned red, and he came to a cautious stop, though no traffic control was needed on the deserted streets and the nearest police were probably holed up in some warm diner. He bent forward, staring through the windshield at the gloom and ugliness of the old street. Even snow and darkness couldn't make anything pleasant of the sordid slums and squalid remains of the former meat-handling plants. Most of the windows were dark, but on the fourth floor of one building lights indicated that the Primates were in session. That didn't mean that anyone would have braved the weather, however; Dave and Tina Hillery would open up anyway, since they lived across the hall in a companion flat. Fred Emmett, whom Harry was supposed to see, was probably home in bed.

Besides, the brief note from the sports car editor had merely said that he'd met Sid Greenwald in Europe and would give details at the meeting of the Primates. There was no indication of anything important; surely even Sid would have cabled if an emergency had come up or if he'd made any real progress in marketing their engine to one of the foreign car makers during the two months he'd been abroad. Sid would hardly have used Emmett as a messenger; the editor was a bore at best, with his fixation on brute power and pure speed, and he'd be even more of a bore now that he'd glutted himself on German and Italian racing designs.

Harry had almost persuaded himself to head for home when the light finally turned green. Then he spotted a parking space nearly free of snow directly in front of the building and reversed his decision. He swung in and cut power. The heater blower slowed to a stop, and he shivered at the suddenly audible whine of the wind outside. He braced himself, threw the door open, and dashed across the rutted ice and into the dimly lighted hallway beyond.

There was a thick stench of mold, cooked cabbage, and soaking clothes. Plaster was cracking from the filthy walls, and the narrow, twisting stairs were sagging and worn. Harry winced; he had a dislike of stairs, and these were completely depressing. Half a flight up, a door had lost its glass and been stuffed with a torn blanket. Now from behind it there came the shriek of a drunken woman's voice raised in foulmouthed anger. It chopped off in mid-speech to the sound of a heavy blow, then picked up in rising stridency. A dog began barking, and there was a scared wailing of children.

Harry shrugged and started up the steps. He'd heard the voice of poverty—or was it merely humanity?—here before. It faded behind him as he twisted his way up the creaking boards. Dim bulbs marked the landings, but all the other doors were dark and silent. One had a cheap, luminescent crucifix fastened to it.

*Henry!*

The voice from his nightmare screamed at him, jolting him and cutting into his mind with a blast of raw fear that froze his lungs and heart. He caught his breath and staggered back a step, tensed with the same horror that had sometimes brought him awake in a cold sweat from his sleep. He had to get out of here! Up there, something foreign to all human feelings was waiting for him, something that must never . . .

Then he mastered it. A trace of dread remained, along with his surprise at being caught by it while awake; the call usually came only in the middle of deep and otherwise dreamless sleep. He took a slow breath, rubbing sweat from his forehead with his sleeve, then started up the stairs again. Most of the reaction had passed by the time he reached the top landing, where a hand-lettered sign indicated the Primates headquarters. From behind the door came a surf-drone of voices that proved the meeting was going on. Apparently the weather had served only as a challenge to bring the members out. There was no way of predicting when there would be a good turnout.

Now he hesitated, suddenly obsessed again with the feeling that he had no business here. But before the unease could master him, he threw back the door and stepped in.

The old apartment was well filled. Smoke was thick in the air, mixing with muggy heat and the odor from kerosene heaters. The smoke, Harry knew, was all from pipes and cigarettes; oddly, these gatherings had never turned into pot parties. The dirty walls and windows had been largely covered with yards of cheap draperies of assorted patterns. Rickety chairs and decrepit couches were lined along the walls of the rooms beyond what had been the kitchen, but half the members were standing, clumped into little groups.

Harry threw his trench coat onto a table where others were piled, just as a small man and a large, heavy-busted girl came from across the hall, dressed in thick layers of sweaters and warm outer coats.

"Hi, Harry," Dave Hillery called happily. "Just in time. We're running out of supplies." He held out a box with a red sign inked onto it: *No representation without taxation.* "How about looking at my typewriter this time? It's skipping all the time now."

Harry nodded, remembering a previous promise, and threw a couple of dollars into the box. The Primates had once been an organization of fantasy writers, complete with stiff dues and a constitution, but that had all worn away. Now Harry and a few others donated the low rent

16

here, and the only expense was for beer. No formal list of membership was kept any longer. Though still composed mostly of writers, artists, and engineers who were interested in fantasy, those who came to the monthly meetings were united only by a common enjoyment of argumentation as the highest form of entertainment. They resembled some of the Greenwich Village groups of a former generation, but there was little of the conscious artiness and stylized unconventionality that constituted most modern Village gatherings.

"Any sign of Fred Emmett?" Harry asked.

Dave grunted something from under the table where he was gathering beer bottles into cartons. Tina's flat face broke into an amused grin as she answered. "Nora Bley's got him in tow. I guess she wants to find out if he learned anything from European women."

"Nope." Dave came erect again and began stacking the cartons onto Tina's stout arms. "He was here, but Nora dragged him off early. Said he'd call you later about Sid. Anything important?"

"Who knows? Probably not." If the message from Sid was a request for more money, it would have to wait; Harry had already sent all that he could pry from Grimes, his guardian under the trust in which his money was held.

Dave nodded and followed Tina out, carrying two extra bottles as his share of the load. The Hillerys usually lacked the money to contribute for beer and made up for it by errand work, probably enjoying the chance to display their self-chosen poverty. Dave was a first-rate artist, but he preferred to turn out forth-class fiction instead, with the obvious approval of Tina for whatever he wanted.

Harry shrugged and headed for the front room, momentarily feeling a last prick of what had hit him on the stairs. But there was no sign of monsters lurking there—only a fairly normal-looking bunch of people, most of whom he'd known for years.

Within a few minutes, however, he realized that his hunch was right and that coming here had been a mistake. He was in no mood for a Primates meeting, and the chief

17

topic wasn't something to change his mind; it seemed to center on some magazine story about telepathy and other psi phenomena—a current fad in science fiction which left him too bored to read the stories.

Even the conversation among the smaller groups seemed dull and all too familiar: ". . . Try using a dozen five-inch speakers in an infinite baffle to cut down the Doppler distortion . . . the way Parrish used his blue in those mountain scenes. I start out with a wash . . . Nora's just looking for security. Something to do with her penis envy. She has to try to destroy every man she meets, hoping she'll find one stronger than she is. If she can crack him, she drops him. If he won't crack, she works harder at it. And she's got more drive . . . both deadlines past, nothing done, and right in the middle of my annual slump. So I made up my mind, no matter what drivel came out, I'd write thirty mechanical pages every day until I had the books. And you know what that editor said? . . . even my analyst wouldn't believe me. No, I mean it. He said my Electra complex didn't fit . . ."

Harry left the last group quickly, remembering his own glancing encounter with the girl. There were things the original Eelctra hadn't known. The arrival of Dave with more beer offered a welcome break, but he couldn't shake his mood. Briefly, he relaxed in listening to a rocket fuel chemist banging away on the battered piano; the man was patching a boogie bass onto a Wagnerian theme and doing a good job of it. But then a highly respected mathematician who had been one of the original members but now rarely attended meetings came over, and the piano was forgotten in some nonsensical argument about telepathy as related to information theory.

Harry got up and moved back to the kitchen, which was another mistake. The room was deserted except for a stoutish stranger in a loud sports jacket and Dr. Philip Lawson, a tall figure with a roughly chiseled face, a black mustache, and a thick head of snow-white hair. Lawson was a regular here, having been sponsored by Dave Hillery after the doctor had managed to save Tina from some female trouble without charging her. He seemed generally

18

well liked, but Harry found his almost excessive friendliness disconcerting; he'd exhausted his excuses to the doctor and started repeating before the frequent calls and invitations had finally stopped.

Lawson looked up, and his deeply etched face broke into a sudden smile. "Harry! Meet Ted Galloway of the *Voice*. Emmett brought him around and then stranded him. Ted, Harry Bronson's the inventor of that new engine—the man Fred was telling you about."

The reporter seemed to be the sort of human cipher that Emmett usually discovered. Harry shook hands rather uncomfortably, aware that Emmett's briefing had probably carried more details on the trust fund that enabled Harry to work on engines than on the seriousness of the work itself.

But Galloway seemed pleasant enough and more interested in the meeting than in whatever he had been told previously ."I'm frankly out of my depth here," he confessed. "So I've been getting a little background from Dr. Lawson."

"Don't let the Primates throw you," Harry suggested, opening another beer. He could remember his own confusion when he'd first been invited to a meeting almost ten years before. "Some of that babble is backed up with solid information, but most of it is just bluff. You get to know which is which after a while. Anyhow, it's all in fun. Talk for talk's sake."

Lawson chuckled with an amiability that didn't match the strained attention in his eyes. "Just what I told him, Harry. I've been filling in what snippets of fact there are on psi—Rhine's work, mostly. Pull up a chair."

Harry groped for another excuse, but was saved by the entrance of Dave. The little man broke in with an account of his troubles with the typewriter Harry had promised to look at. Lawson looked disappointed, then shrugged and turned back to Galloway.

Dave's apartment across the hall was surprisingly cheerful. Cheap but tasteful use of drapes and paint, together with clever lighting, made it the envy of many with far more to work with. It was already occupied by Tina and five others, busy with poker; the game must have been going on for some time, since they were already dealing baseball.

Tina raked in a pot and smiled at Harry. "Want in?"

He shook his head. "Never touch it. I always lose."

That was the literal truth; until he'd given up, he had made a perfect record of invariably guessing the other hands wrong. He followed Dave into the bedroom-office where the ancient Adler stood, accepted Dave's few tools, and then settled down. A single experiment showed that the trouble lay in a misadjusted escapement. He'd never worked on an Adler before, and the ease with which it broke apart for service fascinated him. As he began unscrewing the escapement module, Harry felt at peace for the first time since he'd come here.

He'd begun his education in snooty schools designed to turn him into an ornament to society—a man of considerable charm and no conceivable use to the world. But the Army drafted him and sent him to the motor pool to service engines, possibly because his ignorance of the subject was absolute. And there he discovered that machinery was the one thing for which he had a true passion. When he was released, he switched from Harvard to MIT.

He'd been lucky in having to alter his whole sense of values while he could still make the adjustment, though he hadn't felt very fortunate during his first few months in the Army. He'd gone in as an unformed youth and managed somehow to come out as an adult with the potential for making his own decisions and accepting the results. He hadn't enjoyed the process, of course; but since then he'd seen too many who refused to adjust to the realities of life, and he was generally pleased with himself.

Now he felt a glow of appreciation for the workmanship of the old machine. He hardly looked up when Dave brought him a cup of coffee and a better light. It was a beautiful typewriter, the Adler, though worn and ill used. He was just finishing putting it together after cleaning out the last bit of eraser grit when he heard the pounding of feet down the stairs, indicating that some of the meeting was breaking up. The poker game was still going strong as he washed his hands and headed back for his coat.

Most of the members were gone, but a music session had started in the front room, with a guitar and banjo added to the piano and a trumpet blaring raucously over them. The freedom from complaints about noise was the one good reason for keeping the old place as a meeting hall. The trumpeter jerked a thumb toward the window and swung into a few bars of "Jingle Bells." Harry saw that it was snowing again, fine hard flakes whipping across the ice that had formed from the first fall.

In the middle room, Galloway and Lawson were trying to listen to the news on a portable radio while Dave was shouting into the telephone. The little man's face was worried until he saw Harry. Then he dropped the instrument back onto the cradle and swung around.

"I was just going after you, Harry. Man, it's rough out there. Everything's stalled. How about that front-drive wonder buggy of yours? Will it go?"

Harry nodded. He had snow treads on the front wheels, and the car should handle anything that could be navigated. "Why?"

"Because Manhattan's frozen up tighter than a witch. The subway men are pulling a sick-out to take advantage of this for their stalled contract negotiations. The bus at One Hundred Seventy-eighth Street isn't running—nothing is moving. And Doc Lawson's got to get back to Teaneck. I know it's asking a lot, but—"

Harry groaned to himself, but he knew he was stuck. He'd brought it on himself, too; he'd done too much talking about the wonders of the car after he first got it. He brushed aside Lawson's faint protests, deciding that he might as well appear gracious, however he felt. "What about you, Mr. Galloway?"

"He's coming with me," Lawson answered. "I promised to show him some things he might use in a story. But look, I can put up at a hotel . . ."

He obviously didn't mean it. Harry hoped his own protestations of pleasure sounded a little more sincere. They seemed to work, anyhow; the doctor seized on them with a curious look of delight. Harry buttoned on his coat and waved a general good-bye to those who were still there.

As they creaked down the stairs, the blare of the trumpet faded, and everything was silent except for the snores of a drunken, bloody-nosed man outside the blanket-stuffed door. Harry stepped over him, reaching carefully for the step beyond.

*Henry!*

Only the fact that it was a short half flight saved him. His foot missed the step, and he felt himself lurch downward. Somehow, his flailing arms caught the wall at the bottom landing and kept him from falling onto his face. But the terror that gripped him for long seconds had nothing to do with falling.

Then it began to pass, more quickly this time, and he was aware of the two men supporting him. He shook his head sharply. "I'm all right. Just slipped."

"Could happen to anyone here," Lawson agreed quickly with professional assurance. But the doctor's eyes were searching him, and there was a strange tension in the hands on Harry's arms. "Lucky you caught yourself. Sure you're okay?"

Harry nodded, noticing that the drunk was still undisturbed. He muttered something and headed toward the outside. His heart was pounding, and the sweat on his forehead seemed to freeze as the outer air hit him. But the chilling wind was somehow bracing and normal. His hands were only slightly unsteady as he twisted the key to start the motor. A moment later, he turned on the heater fan and felt the welcome warmth begin drying his damp skin.

Lawson was still studying him, but now seemed to relax. On the back seat, Galloway bounced up and down appreciatively and grunted in pleased surprise. "What kind of car is this, Bronson? And how come you got heat like that? My bus takes fifteen minutes to get any steam."

"It's a Citroën," Lawson answered. "And I gather the heat has something to do with Harry's free-piston engine. He's probably changed the whole car by this time."

Harry's respect for the doctor increased suddenly. But he shook his head, glad to turn his mind to something

22

familiar. "No other changes. Why ruin a good design, just to tinker? But you're right, this is the handmade prototype of our engine."

A free-piston engine fired its fuel between two opposing pistons that did no work themselves, but simply served as a source of superhot exploding gas. That was then allowed to expand somewhat, cooling enough to feed a simple turbine that provided the real power. But an added advantage was that some of the gas could be bypassed to an exchanger that gave almost instant heat. Lawson's guess as to the mechanism showed a clever mind—a far more thorough grasp of mechanical principles than could have been expected from the man's normal conversation.

Now the slush was melting from the windshield, and Harry swung the car out onto the choppy ice of the street, skidding a little until he got the feel of the powdery dust of snow over it; he poured on more power, and the front wheels brought it under control. He turned up Tenth Avenue, traveling with the timed lights, passing occasional trucks or cars that were creeping along with thunking chains. More often, he passed abandoned cars that had skidded or been stuck. As he moved uptown, the snow began thickening in the air.

The bridge was nearly deserted, slick and treacherous, with a nasty wind coming in gusts over the river. Once in New Jersey, though, it was somewhat easier going, since the road had been less chewed up before the freeze. They swept down a curving hill into Teaneck, and Lawson pointed to a neon sign in front of a big house set back from the road, then indicated a driveway. As Harry turned in, he saw that the sign carried Lawson's name.

"The mark of the quack," the man said, with more amusement than bitterness in his voice. "I also pay for a listing in the Manhattan phone book, though I can't practice there. I was a surgeon once—a good one. Now my patients are mostly women over forty. The really sick I send elsewhere; the others get terrifying diagnoses and slow but sure wonder cures only I can give. It pays—it should at my fees—and it may even help them psychologically. So now you know what I am. I suppose you'd rather not come in for a drink?"

It had been a deliberate trap, neatly equating refusal with insult, but Harry could see no way to avoid it decently. "I shouldn't," he said, but he was already getting out of the car.

Lawson muttered something about the housekeeper and maid being asleep and began leading them up a beautifully hand-carved walnut stairway toward his private study. Then for the third time, the nightmare voice screamed in Harry's mind.

*Henry!*

He groped for the balustrade, fighting against the gibbering nonsense not quite voiced in his mind. This time his defense was quicker, and it was over almost at once. But Lawson had seen, and one of the man's arms was around Harry's shoulders. Worry was no longer concealed in his voice, though he wore a touch of his professional smile. "Sinus attack?" he asked, glancing at Harry's slightly misshapen nose.

Harry seized on the explanation, nodding quickly while he moved away from the other's support. Maybe it was sinus trouble, some pressure on a nerve; he'd never been bothered by such things before, but it was more logical than his growing feeling that he was being possessed by . . . "I'm all right now."

"I'll give you something that will fix you up for the moment," Lawson decided as they started upward again. "But you'd better see a doctor—a better doctor than I am now—if this keeps up. In here."

He led them through a door on the second floor into a small sitting room done in white leather and fruitwood, with a bedroom off it. He took their coats, then mixed drinks from a small bar. He added a pinch of some white powder to one glass and handed it to Harry. "Just a mild sedative. It won't hurt you or keep you from driving," he explained.

Harry sipped it doubtfully; but there was no taste of drugs, and the liquor helped to dispel the aftereffects of the

24

waking nightmare. He downed it. The tension began leaving, while a sense of vague well-being replaced it. But there was no feeling of drowsiness. Maybe Lawson knew what he was doing.

The doctor had turned to Galloway and was pointing to a crudely designed device of wood and brass under a glass cover. "The original psionics machine. Magic diagnosis." He lifted the cover and began demonstrating. "Put one drop of the patient's blood—blood is life, you know—one drop in this pan and cover it; it's window dressing to impress him, of course. Rub this rod with a piece of catskin and touch it here; that charges the gold-leaf electroscope until the leaves repel each other and fly apart. Then put one hand on the flat brass plate and make a series of passes across your body—yours, not the patient's, for full magic effect—with the other. When the leaves fall, that's it. Spot the gimmick?"

Galloway was frowning uncertainly, but Harry nodded. "Of course. It works like a crude lie detector. When you think you've hit the trouble, your hand sweats. That lowers your resistance enough for the thing to discharge through you. But who'd fall for it?"

"Most patients. I use one in my office. Of course, I also give a regular examination afterwards, but this is what they pay for. It has also convinced a fair number of men who want to believe in psi."

Harry refilled his glass from the bar, studying the simple device. He'd heard it cited as proof of psionics, but had never seen a model before. It was a relief to find Lawson discussing it frankly. "Another example of the will to believe making fools of observers, eh?" he asked.

"Is it?" Lawson grinned at him, his face sharpening. "Harry, I've diagnosed things with this that I couldn't figure out without it. Not too surprising, of course—it works like a ouija board, bringing out what's in the back of the user's mind. But now tell me how that mind can spot a tumor too small to show on a plate and completely masked by other things that fully account for the symptoms! I consider this little gadget more worthy of study than anything Rhine came up with. You can say it works by bringing out

25

what we know by subliminal observation—but then we'd better study such observations! Too bad I can't demonstrate it for you. But as I promised Ted, I can show you Rhine's main test. Here."

He dragged a deck of cards from a drawer and spread them. There were five each of five simple symbols—cross, circle, and such. "Pure guesswork should give you five right guesses to the pack. Want to try it, Ted? Harry can deal them and you call them out while I check. Run through it three times and let's see what score you get."

Harry had started to rise, putting his drink down; he had no desire to fool with any of the rigmarole. But the cards were in his hands before he could protest. Lawson stepped back with paper and pencil, gesturing for him to start, and Galloway was waiting. Damn it . . .

Then he began dealing while Galloway called and Lawson checked the answers against the cards. It was over sooner than he'd expected, and Galloway turned his eyes toward the doctor with a plainly hopeful expression.

Lawson shook his head. "Fourteen—within normal limits for guesswork. Ted, you can put down your reporting hunches as superstition. You're a neutral as far as psi goes, at least by this test. Want to get even by testing Harry here?"

Seeing the hurt look on Galloway's face, Harry made no protest at changing places. It was only fair, after all. Anyhow, while the results would be only chance, no matter what they showed, this test was elementary and not like some of the mumbo jumbo involved in most of the discussions he'd heard. He tried honestly to let his mind relax and began calling whatever came to him first.

Lawson totaled the score without expression while Galloway refilled their glasses. Then the doctor dropped into the chair opposite Harry, wiggling his metallic pencil slowly back and forth. "I didn't have to count, this time. An absolute blank—not one correct answer," he said.

Galloway was obviously pleased. So was Harry.

"I guess that proves I'm a complete blank to psi," he said, trying to make a joke of it.

"If it isn't blind luck—and that's just too good a
26

negative score—it proves you're loaded for bear with psi powers," Lawson told him. Galloway frowned, but the doctor nodded. "That's right. A negative score is as important as a positive one. It indicates the mind can tell, but is either hiding from itself or covering up for some reason. Otherwise, you'd be bound to get a few right. Were you ever a wonder child? Learn to talk or read at some incredible age—things like that?"

"No," Harry answered. Then he signed. Inevitably, sooner or later something always came up that made telling the truth necessary, and he should have been used to it by now. "I don't know. My parents died in a wreck, so I'm told, but I can't remember them. I seem to remember a fire—maybe the car burned—but nothing before that. I was ten then, and my first real memory is of my guardian coming to visit me in the hospital and telling me I had nothing to worry about! I've had a mess of psychological probing, but nobody could do anything about my memory. Those first ten years are simply a blank."

At least Lawson had enough sense not to start oozing sympathy about something that was long ago and now only unemotionally connected with Harry. He nodded. "Traumatic amnesia. Rare—most cases are faked—but it does happen, and it's sometimes permanent. I wonder if that has anything to do with your complete negative attitude toward psi? A block set up, perhaps, because you got a presentiment before the accident, confused cause and effect, and have been blaming yourself for what happened. I could probably find out if you'd let me hypnotize you and erase the block—something a lot easier than trying to cure your amnesia. Care to look at this pencil and let me try?"

"No!"

"All right." Lawson seemed to accept it as something to be expected. "Then keep your eyes off the pencil, Harry. Because something bright like the pencil moving back and forth, back and forth like this, is about the most hypnogenetic thing there can be. That's the way hypnotism works. You find your full attention centered on something like this pencil moving back and forth and the first thing you know, you can't look away. And it's easy to let your

27

mind drift as it moves back and forth . . . and you know what's happening, but you don't care. Of course, until you feel sleepy, you're completely safe . . . Safe to relax . . . The pencil will only make you feel a little sleepy . . . comfortably sleepy . . . It's easy to be sleepy here where it's so safe . . . so safe and sleepy . . ."

Harry knew he was being hypnotized. He never fully lost consciousness, but he relaxed further, feeling deliciously sleepy and safe. There was even a kind of familiar feeling about it. He heard Lawson's voice and answered casually. Then there was a lot more comfortable speech by Lawson about how he could see the right answers, and how the block in his mind was just something he'd grown out of, and how it couldn't help him, and how he could see that it was much easier to tell the whole truth. It was all very assuring and comfortable, and there was nothing to which he could object. A part of his mind even realized that his worry about posthypnotic commands was just silly, because Lawson was giving no such commands. He was fully aware of being hypnotized, but he rather liked it. Lawson, he decided lazily, was pretty darned good at this. He must have said it aloud, because Lawson was agreeing. Then, at a quiet suggestion that he was fully awake now, he found himself alert again, under the scrutiny of a puzzled Galloway and a smiling Lawson.

The doctor put the pencil away. "A dirty trick, Harry. I set you up for it. But I warned you that I have no medical ethics. And I'm curious about how well you can do positively on a test now. How about it? Or would you rather get mad and pound me to a pulp?"

Harry swore softly to himself. Then he laughed wryly. "All right, I walked into your trap. And I'm suddenly curious, too. So bring on your damned test."

This time the test was more elaborate. Lawson gave Galloway a box and sent him into the bedroom to shuffle the cards, then seal them back in the box. When the closed box was returned, he handed pencil and paper to Harry with instructions to write whatever came to his mind and keep writing until he drew a blank. This was clairvoyance, not telepathy, and they'd check the results when they opened the box; until then, nobody would know the real order of the cards.

Harry stared at the paper, trying to picture some simple symbol. Nothing came. Instead, he could think of only the two of spades. He frowned, then grinned and wrote that down. He'd write down any crazy ideas he had and see what it did to the test. Anyhow, that fitted his instructions. He lifted the pencil—and a diamond five was in his mind. This time he hesitated. But Lawson could very well have used a different sort of deck—a thicker one, perhaps, so that Harry might have noted the difference unconsciously. He wrote down a joker next, then went on more rapidly, not counting. When no more pictures came, he handed Lawson the paper.

"Canasta deck?" he asked. Galloway's face changed color, but Lawson only nodded.

"You could have guessed that from hearing some faint sound of the shuffle—a double deck is hard to handle," the doctor said. "Let's see what we find in the box before we give you credit."

The first card was the deuce of spades, the next the five of diamonds, the third a joker. By the fifth card, Harry was sweating. By the tenth, his stomach was sick and cold. There were a hundred and eight cards in the box. And finally, on the paper before him, there were one hundred and eight check marks indicating correct answers.

"What are the mathematical odds against that?" Lawson asked quietly.

Harry's mind tried to figure it briefly. It was some astronomical sum—an unreal sum. More unreal than even the possibility of clairvoyance. More unreal than certain evil . . .

"I want to go home," he heard himself cry, and it was the sound of a small and lost child. He was already on his feet, moving through the door and across to the stairway. His foot took a single step before Lawson could reach him and restrain him. "I want to go home."

"All right, my boy, we'll take you home." Lawson's voice came from some incredibly great and alien distance. But it no longer mattered.

Something in Harry's mind seemed to contract to a small, tight tunnel and then go zooming outward. It landed against coldness that was hard and impenetrable and ricocheted back at him.

*Henry!*

And something else in his mind screamed and ran down another tunnel and away, gibbering through infinity and into the infinitesimal. He staggered, groping for Lawson helplessly, then collapsed on the stairs, throwing up with violent contractions of his stomach as he lost consciousness.

## III.

### SLANT

Ted Galloway hadn't seen the dawn for a long time. Not since City College with that girl—what was her name?—the one that married the rich kid from Colgate. Back then he'd even written a couple of verses about dawn, rather pretty poems as he remembered. That was before he'd learned that poetry was no longer supposed to be pretty; the stuff had to have the right slant for the established circle of poets—the ones who made their money writing books about each other. He hadn't been their type, of course.

He sighed tiredly and turned to glance back where young Bronson was sprawled on the rear seat. The kid still seemed to be asleep. Whatever the drug had been that Lawson used, it must have packed a wallop. Like the stuff the doctor had prescribed for Galloway's hangover. He still felt a little disconnected, but his stomach and head were all right now.

Then his eyes went back to the sight of the bridge through the windshield of the Citroën. It looked different in the dawn. There was a soft transparency to colors and a blending of outlines that he had almost forgotten. "Corot," he muttered to himself.

Lawson seemed not to have heard as he slowed the car to drop money into the toll basket. But he nodded as they began moving onto the lower level. There was little traffic, but the roads were still a mess; yet he was handling the unfamiliar car almost casually already.

"You're right—it is like some of Corot's paintings," he agreed with none of the amused condescension most men in his income class would show to a two-bit columnist who talked about art. "Did you get your story, Ted?"

Galloway grimaced unhappily. "Sure, if I want to use it. Fake doctor who advertises uses kook machines on menopausal women. Cynical, of course, the way most of my columns are supposed to be."

"All right," Lawson told him. "Use my name, if you want. It won't hurt me. Most of my patients are already warned against me, but they flock in, anyhow."

Galloway sighed. Once in a while he had a rush of ethics to the head. He couldn't ridicule a man he liked. Fake or not, Lawson seemed to be a right guy. After the boy flipped from the excitement of hitting that jackpot of results, Lawson had sat up all night with him; at least he'd been up soothing the kid's delirious babbling when Galloway awoke to go to the bathroom.

Drat it, there was no way he could find a slant for any other story from the night, however. The Primates had turned out to be a lot more normal than that pompous Emmett had led Galloway to believe; they might be nuts, but they lacked the color he needed. And he couldn't slip any of that card test stuff past his editor without a thousand signed testimonials that it had happened. The old man's bag was astrology, not cards. There was no slant on that which he could see.

"Just how do you figure the odds against a perfect run like that?" he asked.

Lawson shrugged. "It doesn't matter—they're too big. Though in theory, there's as good a chance the first time as there is the gigillionth. But I sometimes think the mathematicians are on the wrong track, and that the so-called laws of chance are based on pure superstition. They don't seem to work consistently. What's a perfect hand for rubber bridge?"

"Eh? Thirteen spades, I suppose."

"You can do better. Ten of a suit to the ace, king, queen—and the other three aces. Put all the other honors in one opponent's hand. Assuming you're vulnerable, you get better than twenty-five hundred points for a grand slam in no trump, doubled and redoubled. It's no fun playing, since it's a laydown. But it's quite a hand, and the odds against it are pretty high. Yet I knew a lawyer named Charles Grimes who got it twice in one year."

"You think that stunt with the cards was just wild coincidence, then?" Galloway asked.

Lawson shrugged again as he turned the car south on West End Avenue. "I'd rather not think. I learned about mathematics and coincidence when I was young enough to believe in absolutes. I learned a lot about medical ethics at the same time, and it took several years of experience before I matured enough as a physician to have doubts. Then I did some things I'd once have crucified any other man for doing. Nothing is as sure as we'd like."

"That run of predictions was pretty absolute."

"So it seemed. Call it coincidence, or find a better answer. But do you really think a man who could do a thing like that would let anyone test him? He wouldn't want it known, and he'd have better things to do with his ability than to play card tricks with me or with Rhine's group."

It made sense, and Galloway was conscious of a sudden relief. Then he frowned to himself. He was already late with his column, and it had to be in by noon. Maybe, if he called up an actuary he knew and used last night against the statistics he'd get, he might cook up a story. It was at least some kind of slant. Most of his readers would enjoy seeing any expert put down.

Anyhow, that business of things coming in threes was supposed to be superstition, but he'd seen it work much too often. And he'd once won a five-horse parlay the day after winning the daily double; it had paid for a year in Paris, trying to do a serious book. Nothing had come of that, but

. . .

They were in the low Seventies now, and Lawson slid into an empty space before a solid old apartment building. "We're here," he announced.

Bronson was still apparently asleep, but he stirred as Lawson opened the back door and spoke to him. His face remained expressionless, but he followed orders exactly. His eyes opened, and he climbed out, to walk beside the doctor like an automaton, into the building and then to an elevator.

"He acts like a zombi," Galloway commented.

Lawson's mouth twisted into a bitter smile. "For the moment," he said, "he *is* a zombi. The drug I gave him was originally used for making what men called the walking dead, though I've purified it so that I can standardize the dose. It's harmless enough for a while, and it will give him time to recover. I've done a lot of research on odd drugs since—since I became what I am." He took the key from Bronson and opened the door to an apartment, then headed for the bedroom with the young man.

Galloway stared around, whistling softly to himself as the place registered on his mind. The apartment was no bigger than his own dump, but there was no other similarity. This spelled money and casual, unostentatious taste. He could slave all his life without getting what the kid had without doing a stitch of work. Still, it was no sweat off his nose, though he'd have liked a couple of the paintings on the wall.

"Bronson be all right alone?" he asked as Lawson finally came out.

"He'll be all right until I can look in on him again." But there was a strain around the doctor's eyes as he looked back toward the door he'd closed. "There's more than just what happened with the cards, Ted—as I should have discovered before I tried that on him. From his babblings, I gather he's been—well, call it hagridden. If something isn't done about that now, he'll be in real trouble. Damn it, I'm a fool; only a fool uses hypnotism without knowing all the facts. Can I give you a lift somewhere?"

Galloway blinked at the change of subject. "In what?"

"In Harry's car. I'm borrowing it, since it's the best one I
34

can find for the roads now. I've got to make a trip upstate to a private sanatorium, it seems. But I've got enough time to run you downtown."

Galloway thanked him, but set off on foot for the Broadway bus, using the excuse that the cold air would clear his head. Somehow, he couldn't see himself asking Lawson to stop somewhere so he could get the *Morning Telegraph* before he reached the office.

It was a good thing, as it turned out. There was a horse listed as Last Slant that was a twenty to one shot. Galloway had a hunch his luck was about to change.

# IV.

## HUNCH

The telephone woke Harry, but it had already stopped ringing by the time he could recognize the sound for what it was. He opened his eyes slowly, to see daylight poking between the blinds of his bedroom. He felt tired, as if he'd been up all night working on some tough design, and there seemed to be a layer of cotton wool around his thoughts.

Then it began to clear, and memory of the events before he'd passed out came creeping back, along with a faint certainty that Lawson and Galloway had driven him back and put him to bed. Funny, that parlor trick of Lawson's somehow stacking the deck had really hit him, though he knew several magicians who could probably duplicate it. He must have been drinking more than he realized. But he felt no hangover. In fact, he was beginning to feel surprisingly good, as if some dark pressure had suddenly lifted from his mind.

The telephone began to ring again, and he reached for it. "Hello, Phil."

Lawson's voice was carefully jovial and amused. "So you're finally awake, Harry. Know what day this is?"

"Sure. Monday morning."

"Make it Wednesday morning. You've been sedated for the past forty-eight hours. But you looked pretty good when I dropped by last night, so I figured you'd be in shape today. How do you feel?"

"Good." He began apologizing for all the trouble he'd made, but the doctor cut him off.

"My own fault, darn it. I should have spotted that touch of fever you had before I pulled that fool hypnotism stunt on you. I warned you I wasn't much of a real physician anymore. You were in no condition to have silly tricks worked on you. Anyhow, I borrowed your car, so I'm probably in your debt." Lawson's voice suddenly sobered and grew more professional. "You should be all right now, Harry, but take it easy. Eat a good breakfast—and take a lot of salt with it—and then stay home and loaf around today. There shouldn't be any trouble, but if you feel the slightest touch of dizziness, give me a call. I'll be here all day in the office. I left the number, though you could find it in your book, you know. Okay?"

Harry thanked him again and prepared to follow his advice about breakfast. The kitchen showed evidence of someone having used it. Lawson must have fixed food for him while he was under drugs, but the dishes had been washed and put away more or less correctly. Harry started the coffee and then went in search of a deck of cards, shuffling them while his eggs poached. Then he sat down with paper and pencil to make a list while he ate.

Getting any feeling for the cards seemed difficult this time, and he had to count to be sure he had fifty-two listed. When he checked against the deck, he found three correct answers. That seemed a little higher than pure chance, but not wildly so. Certainly there was no proof of precognition involved. He sighed softly and put the cards away, finally convinced that Lawson had pulled a good bit of amateur magic on him.

The mail and papers were waiting, and he saw that it really was Wednesday. Nothing seemed very important, though there was a galley of Galloway's next column in one envelope. He glanced at it and found it reasonably accurate in the little that dealt with him; it seemed that Galloway had been taken in by Lawson, too—which was probably what the doctor had intended. The rest of the column was typical of a layman's attempt to debunk probability theory and not very well done. He tossed the mail aside and decided it was a good day to find out why his tape recorder had suddenly developed an unpleasant amount of distortion.

The phone interrupted him again, just as he was delicately maneuvering a tension spring back onto its peg. His hand jerked, and the spring vanished somewhere into the works. He swore softly and went to pick up the phone.

"Hi, Nettie. How's Florida?"

There was a sharp gasp from the phone. "How'd you know? How did you know where I've been? Even my husbad didn't guess. Harry, if you've been putting a spy on me—"

That, he admitted to himself, was an excellent question. While he fumbled his way to some kind of answer, he suddenly remembered that he'd also known the other call was from Lawson before he'd heard the doctor's voice.

In the end, she seemed to forget it, largely because she was so full of her recent decision to get a divorce that nothing else mattered. He listened with appropriate responses while she went on and on. He finally got free by offering to defrost a couple of steaks that evening if she wanted to come up to talk.

But as he went back to the tape recorder, he was still mulling over her question. Drat it, guessing Lawson's call could be explained; the doctor would logically have wanted to find how he felt. But Nettie was another matter. If he'd known she'd left town, he might have guessed that she would visit her mother; but if he had guessed that, why should he have expected her to call him this morning? Unless there was something about her breathing that he could recognize over the phone . . .

He was careful the next time to wait before using the caller's name. But it was only Fred Emmett on the phone, with nothing important concerning his meeting with Sid Greenwald; rather than pass along information, the man was intent on pumping him for details on what the new compression ratios would mean to racing.

Dinner with Nettie proved to be a minor mistake; with a

somewhat estranged but highly solvent husband, she'd been addlepated but enjoyable company. Now, having opted for freedom, there was something a little too calculating in the way she surveyed him and his apartment. But his adolescent horror of being bored by people had long since been moderated by experience. He let her chatter on until midnight before getting rid of her. Then he shoved the dishes into the dishwasher, made a few quick tests on the reassembled recorder, and decided to turn in. Tomorrow would be when the trouble started . . .

He cut the thought off, swearing at his mind. Damn it, was he still kidding himself that he might have precognition?

But his last thought was a certainty that there would be no nightmares and no voices calling his name. In that, he was right, though he had a dull feeling of something reaching toward his mind, something with ideas that had no business in his head. He turned over, half waking, and it seemed to go away.

The next morning began well enough. Lawson called and seemed pleased at Harry's report. Galloway made what seemed to be a sincere inquiry about his health. And Tina Hillery wanted to kid him about the column in the *Voice*. Well, he'd laced into her once about her astrology craze, and turnabout was only fair. Besides, she always had a supply of good-natured gossip about the doings of various Primates. He was chuckling when he finally hung up the phone.

But tension began to build up over his second cup of coffee. He tried to shake it off, but his rationality was at a low ebb. Apparently, once the mind had any evidence it could perform miracles, it refused to give up the idea and started trying to prove itself. Now if anything unpleasant developed, it could claim more proof; if nothing happened, it could simply wait until something did. No wonder it was so hard to shake the faith of less rational kooks. Next he'd be switching from coffee to tea so he could read the leaves!

Something suddenly nagged at his mind then. Tea . . . But he couldn't trace the idea and went back to general worrying.

He was hovering over the phone when it rang again, and he caught it at the first sound. But there was no risk of anticipating the caller's identity; the voice was snapping out as he got the receiver to his ear.

"Henry? Charles Grimes here. What the devil's all this stuff my office sent over? They've got your name on some piece about fortune-telling. We can sue 'em for things like that. Or can we?"

"I'm afraid not, Uncle Charles." There was no blood relationship, but the courtesy title had become a habit. "Galloway's report was accurate enough as far as it went. Anyhow, there's no harm—"

"No harm? No harm!" Grimes was in an obvious raging tizzy. Then his voice dropped as if he were exerting some tremendous control over it. "All right, Henry. All right. I guess you would feel that way. You wouldn't know. But I think you'd better get up here. And don't be all day about it! We've got some talking to do."

"Half an hour," Harry agreed, and hung up before he could hear the certain protest against any delay at all. He poured himself another coffee and took it to the bathroom with him. He had no intention of appearing before Grimes' ward, Ellen Palermo, with a stubble of beard, and besides, a little waiting might remind the old man that he couldn't issue imperious orders any longer.

During all the twenty years Harry could remember, Grimes had been the voice of authority. It had been Grimes who told a frightened amnesiac boy the ugly facts of his life, Grimes who had picked his schools and for a time even guided his thoughts. But it had never been a peaceful relationship. Even during his youthful period of rebellion against his elders, Harry had usually realized that the old man did his honest duty as he saw it; but something about him grated on Harry's nerves, and he was sure the reverse was true. Since the big battle over Harry's switch from law to engineering, they had seen as little as possible of each other.

Unfortunately, it had worked out that he also saw less of Ellen. She'd been a ward of Grimes since before Harry was left to the old man, but both had been away at school most of the time until Harry came back from the Army. Then he'd found the saucy and plaguing girl-child changed into an amazingly attractive woman. She could never be called beautiful; but there was a vividness to her brunette looks, and her occasional smile had hit him hard at first. For a little time, Harry had thought it was mutual.

Then she had pulled back into a shell. Somehow, she was always too busy to see him, except in chance meetings or when he came to see Grimes. He was sure there was no other man, and she didn't seem to dislike him; but there was a strain between them, obviously. He blamed that on the influence of Grimes, though he had no evidence of his suspicions.

Still, sometimes when he called on the old lawyer, he was able to wangle a dinner date from her, and since this might be one of those times, he meant to look his best.

Grimes owned the building where Harry lived. He occupied a large apartment on the top floor, serviced by a private elevator. He still maintained a law office in the financial district but spent most of his time at home, where Ellen had gradually taken over most of the work as his secretary.

Grimes answered the buzzer himself, and Harry saw that this didn't seem to be one of the lucky times; there was no sign of the girl. But the lawyer gave him no time to inquire. "You took long enough!"

Harry started to make an automatic crack and then killed it. The old man didn't look well. His short figure was thinner than ever, and the skin of his face was like stretched parchment. Only his wild shock of gray hair was normal, and even that was receding now, Harry noticed for the first time.

"Sorry, Uncle Charles," he said.

Grimes sniffed, but seemed somewhat relieved at even the token apology. He led the way into his office and gestured to a chair beside the desk. For a moment after he took his own seat, he seemed uncertain. He pawed at the clipping from the *Voice*, then shoved it away. His thin lips tightened. Then he fished a yellowed slip of paper from one drawer and handed it to Harry.

41

"Your mother and her partner," he said. "They had the greatest act of stage mentalism ever seen. That was taken when she announced she was quitting to marry your father. I once hoped—but that's no business of yours."

Harry had never seen a picture of his mother. He studied the old clipping from some magazine, surprised that he could find no emotion at seeing this first real evidence of her existence. It was only a rather pretty woman's image to him. It related to the ten years completely lost to his memories and emotions, not to what had become his real life. His eyes dropped to the caption: "Palermo and Lavalle to Fold!"

"Palermo!" he exclaimed.

Grimes nodded. "Nick Palermo—Ellen's father and the best friend I ever had. He died in a home for the criminally insane—sent there for having strangled a wife he deeply loved! Don't tell me there's no harm in all this extrasensory rigmarole!"

"But theirs was stage mentalism," Harry protested. "It has nothing to do with—"

"The hell it doesn't!" Grimes' hands were shaking as he snatched the picture back and shoved it into the drawer. There were two bright spots of red on his pale cheeks. "They believed in it. That's the devilish danger of the stuff —it's like opium! At first, you just play with it—and then it owns you. Even I began to believe in it. They started making a life around it. Palermo and Bronson, and then they found others. I was just a lawyer acting as their investment adviser at first. Then they had a little colony. And then—then it was gone. Ugly, ugly! And I came back here with two kids to keep in trust and protect."

He shoved back the chair and stood beside the desk, bent so that his hands could grasp the edge until the knuckles were white. "No harm? Henry, your mother had a vision of what was going to happen. But did it save her? It did not! Because she had to have it happen that way or it meant her vision was wrong—and she cared more about her so-called powers than anything else. She *made* it happen the way she saw it. She had to! And if you start fooling with this stuff . . ."

42

Harry had been listening with a mixture of shock at the revelations and a growing sympathy for Grimes' obvious disturbance. But the last sentence snapped him out of it, reminding him that Grimes had once had a reputation as a trial lawyer, where he could sway jurors with emotional asides that somehow always came back to the point he wanted to make.

"I wasn't fooling with anything," he began.

"And you're not going to fool with anything!" Grimes jerked the chair back and perched on it again, his black eyes snapping at Harry. "You'll have nothing—absolutely nothing—to do further with any fortune-telling, extrasensory nonsense, or whatever. No gambling. No display for any stupid reporters. And no contact with this Lawson. Oh, I know him. He was a fine physician once—before he took up kookery. Now he's no fit person for you to associate with."

"Or?"

"Or you'll find yourself cut off without another penny from the trust." Grimes grinned thinly, a tightening of his lips that displayed clenched teeth. "You know damned well that I control every cent for you—to do as I choose, unless and until I relinquish control or die. I can cut you off, and don't you think I can't. Oh, you might get a court order to have it turned over to you—but I could stall it off for years. Years! You either give me your promise to drop this nonsense immediately—or you'll be too busy trying to keep bread in your mouth to have any time left for it."

"Am I supposed to let you pick all my friends from now on?" Harry asked with elaborate calm. He could feel the blood rushing angrily to his face while his stomach was cold and hard, but he tried to keep his voice level.

"Reject friends you shouldn't have, yes." The grin widened. "Oh, not your so-fast friend Greenwald. You'll have to reject him yourself, unless he has enough to pay his way back from Europe. So far, you've drawn a sizable fortune for that toy engine of yours and for Greenwald to waste promoting it. I've never said a word—"

"You've said a lot of words on that!"

"I've never said a word—other than some good advice—to prevent your playing inventor. But if you go against me now, that gets cut off, too. Henry, I won't have you turn out like Ellen!"

"What happened to Ellen?" Harry asked quickly.

"Never mind. She left—months ago. And don't go trying to find her. She's another person I won't have you seeing!"

"So you bullied your little slave once too often," Harry guessed. "A great job our fathers did in picking a guardian for us. Though I suppose they didn't know how far you'd go in playing the dictator."

Grimes leaned forward, his mouth opening. Then he forced himself back, as if swallowing something that was bitter to his taste. "Your father knew, young man. He was rational enough for a while after—after what happened. It was *his* idea then that you were never to have anything to do with these extrasensory affairs. I'm only following my promise to him. I promised—and I keep my word."

"You've got his instructions in writing, I suppose," Harry suggested.

"No." Suddenly Grimes seemed to relax, and his head nodded faintly. His smile was almost approving. "The point is yours. But my point is that I can and will cut you off unless you obey my wishes on this. Well?"

"You," Harry told him, "can go to hell!"

Grimes nodded again. "I'm quite aware of that from long experience. Unfortunately, the road may be even easier for you . . . You can let yourself out, Henry."

Harry's first reaction barely lasted until he reached his apartment. The trouble was that he really had no wish to disobey. He had neither liking nor experience for gambling—even the stock market left him completely bored. He hadn't the faintest idea of how to go about approaching the real psi cultists. There was no reason for him to seek the company of Dr. Lawson, however kind the man might have been after the initial trouble. And he didn't know where Ellen might be. It seemed that he might well wind up following Grimes' instructions for lack of ability to do otherwise.

Harry was also intelligent enough to have a fair idea of what a poor prospect he would be to support himself. True, he had a valid degree in engineering, but having done nothing with it since graduation would look strange to any potential employer. Even if he got a job, he probably would not be able to hold it; he'd never developed the work habits needed for gainful employment. He could work like a fool at something he wanted to do, but he doubted that he could keep his mind on anything routine.

He had no need to check his bank balance. It had grown during his time in the Army, but most of the reserve had disappeared when he decided to send Sid to Europe. He might be able to live for six months on what was left—provided no emergency came up.

The emergency had already come, he found on opening his mail. There was a letter from Greenwald asking for additional money.

There was also a raft of crank mail from people who had seen Galloway's column and been smart enough to look for his address in the phone book. He plowed through a few of the pitiful, irrational ravings and barely scanned the rest. Were there really that many lonely, ineffectual people whose only hope lay in finding miracles within themselves? Did they have to have God-like powers to prove that they were not merely animals, as they seemed to fear?

Only one letter puzzled him. The writer had circled part of the column and neatly inked the margin with a comment. It said simply: "God have mercy on you, Mr. Bronson." It was signed: "A fellow victim."

It might have been another crank note, except for what happened as he read it. There was a sudden cry in a woman's voice in his head and a feeling of tears on his face. A vague terror reached him, to be quelled almost instantly. Faintly, words seemed to form. "Help us. Oh, God, help us both. Don't let *them* get us!"

Then it was gone. His fingers, touching his face, found no trace of the tears he had felt so distinctly.

Psychic—or psychotic? He shook his head. Damn Grimes! The man had obviously been trying to suggest that the pursuit of the first state created the second. Hearing imaginary voices in his head would be plainly psychotic, seeming to prove the point. Yet the idea simply didn't agree

45

with the number of mediums who died at advanced ages with no greater degree of insanity than they'd had initially. Nettie consulted an old crone who seemed to believe she could foresee the future part of the time, and her only obvious psychosis lay in her excessive need for alcohol.

Still, he was aware that he was developing a nagging feeling that he might be able to exercise powers beyond the normal, and that fitted with Grimes' idea that the need for the psychic became an obsession. How much evidence did he have, one way or another?

He could dismiss the calling of the cards; they could have been stacked somehow, or it could have been a miracle of coincidence, but he had no way of evaluating it. There had been the awareness of the identity of his callers; that could be explained, perhaps, but the explanations required too many wild speculations. He'd had a hunch that today would bring trouble; most days did, though it hadn't been as bad as he'd expected; anyhow, he should have known that Grimes would be upset by the publicity, whatever the man's reasons.

It all added up to nothing, one way or the other. So the only sane and rational thing was to put it to a test where he couldn't know the answer but would be interested enough in the outcome to make his mind work. Then, if he got the right answer, he'd have reason to check further; if he drew a blank, he could forget the whole thing.

He knew the question: Where was Ellen Palermo? There were probably ways of tracing her, but why bother if he could find the answer by hunch?

He pictured her in his mind, trying to fill in a background that would offer a clue. Or a number, a street sign, some building. Then he tried turning in the chair, seeking to find a direction that seemed right.

After fifteen minutes, he gave up. The trouble was not that nothing came—rather, it was that he could force backgrounds, numbers, directions, and words, but there was no meaning or pattern to it. His head had begun to ache with the strain. He made himself a fresh pot of coffee—he was drinking too much coffee, of course—and took a couple of aspirins. His head still felt strange, as if he'd sprained a brain cell or two, but the pain faded.

Then he got out a big map of the city and spread it on the floor. With his eyes closed, he began crawling about on it, trying to use a pencil like a dowsing rod. His first mark was in the middle of the Hudson River, and for a moment he had a horrible reaction to that. Then he conquered his alarm and tried again. Eventually, he had most of the map spotted with marks that were obviously randomized around a central point. As a dowser, it seemed, he was a total failure.

With a mixture of relief and a strange reluctance, he put the map away. So he wasn't psychic. He'd simply had a rush of rubbish to the head. And the longer he stayed holed up here, the worse it would get.

He found his keys finally on the sideboard where Lawson must have dropped them, slipped on a light coat, and took the elevator down to the garage. The car had been washed free of the grime and salt from the roads, and he saw that the tank was full of gas. In some ways, at least, Phil Lawson was an admirable man; no one with a respect for machinery could be all bad.

As he wheeled the Citroën out onto the street, he found that most of the snow and ice were already gone. The weather had turned clear and much warmer. With no particular object in mind, he headed south, figuring on taking the Lincoln Tunnel out to New Jersey and perhaps dropping by the workshop to see if the new casting he'd ordered had been delivered.

Within the first ten blocks of driving, he was sure that the tan Volkswagen in his rearview mirror was following him. He picked the next eastbound street and crossed it to Broadway, with the tan car still behind him. Damn it, he should have guessed that Grimes would be thorough enough to have all his movements followed until Harry promised to obey the latest dicta. While there was no reason to conceal his visit to his shop, he didn't at all fancy the idea of being spied on.

Harry moved over to Ninth Avenue and headed down until he was in the maze of the Village. There he cruised at random for perhaps ten minutes. The other car stayed with him, and he began to realize that he had no clear idea of how to shake it.

Abruptly, he braked and swung right. He took a sharp left, then another right. In the middle of a block, he turned into an alley that he hadn't known was there and followed it without hesitation to what seemed a dead end. At the last minute, a side alley showed, and he managed to turn left into it. A few minutes later, he was heading for an entrance to the West Side Highway, Northbound. There was no sign of his follower.

Harry grinned to himself. He hadn't the faintest notion of exactly what he'd managed to do back there or whether he had gone the wrong way on a one-way street. It had simply felt right, and it had worked. Maybe his study of the map had helped—or maybe . . .

He let that thought die. He'd made his test and drawn a blank. No more psychic nonsense for him now!

He was too busy remembering the way the car had behaved in escaping pursuit to notice the Forty-Second Street exit. He shrugged. It didn't matter. Maybe he'd take the bridge across the river; it was a longer route, but one surer to defeat any follower, in case the tan car was still casting about in hopes of finding him.

As usual, there was a pileup of cars on the highway, and he was forced to sit while the police finally came and managed to clear it up. He began thinking about Ellen again, and his thoughts were not too pleasant. He'd always assumed that Grimes had legally adopted her. The idea of her being on her own with little more background for supporting herself than he had wasn't a happy one.

He could put a notice in the Personal section, but he was reasonably sure that she'd never see it. Grimes would find out about it, however. So that was no solution. There must be some way to trace a young woman who had to find employment, even in a city as large as New York. But he hadn't the faintest idea of how to go about it.

It was quite a bit later that he suddenly thought of Galloway. Of course! The columnist might not know how to find her, but he could surely locate someone who would know.

He'd seemed genuinely friendly and would probably be glad to help.

With that solved for the moment, Harry put it out of his mind and began to wonder where he was. He'd obviously not taken the bridge, though he couldn't quite understand how he'd missed it.

The toll booth identified the route. He was on the New England Thruway, already in Connecticut!

For a moment he was annoyed. Then he grinned at himself. He had only been driving to get out of the apartment, after all. He might as well go on along this route as any other. He remembered a rather pleasant restaurant in Wallingford. He could stop there to eat before heading back; by the time the dinner was finished the traffic should be tolerable again. It wasn't exactly a scenic drive, but the worst was already behind him.

It obviously wasn't his day, however, or something strange had happened to the road signs. He had meant to turn to get onto Route 15, but he wound up on 91. He could probably find some dirt road across—and promptly get lost, judging by what had been happening—or go on to Meriden and then backtrack. But by the time he considered that, he was beginning to realize he had somehow overlooked lunch.

"Okay, Suzy," he told the Citroën. "Potluck. We're stopping at the next eating place I see."

It didn't look bad when he drew up to the parking lot. There were a fair number of cars, many of them expensive, and the restaurant had been adapted from what must have been an old mansion—as was true of a number of quite good inns in this area.

It wasn't until he was inside and being seated by a quaint and carefully charming hostess that he recognized what he'd gotten into. It was one of those places that used a lot of excess letters to make it seem old-timey, with a menu in imitation Old English—carefully filled in with a nice modern type so no mistakes could be made. With not too much experience, he guessed that it must do a fine business in ladies' luncheons and similar cultural events. It called itself a Tea Roome and specialized in elaborate cocktails.

Surprisingly, however, the soup was good and honest. And the rolls were fresh and warm. Harry decided that perhaps serendipity had struck again and began to relax.

Behind him, there was a bustle and sliding of chairs as another group was seated. He shuddered mildly at the cocktails that were being ordered and hastily motioned to the waitress to refill his own scotch and water.

"Wait till you try this one," the nasal voice of the woman who had done most of the ordering was ranting on. "I mean, don't judge by all those others. I *know* how simply dreadful they usually are. All full of such silly things. But she's—oh, I mean she must be *psychic*! She just has to be a real gypsy. I mean, how else could she tell Wilbur about his brother? And my ring. I hunted *everywhere* for it. And when the plumber found it, even Wilbur admitted . . ."

The rather pretty young waitress arrived then with Harry's club steak, but he'd heard enough. "Do I gather you have some kind of fortune-teller working here?" he asked.

"Yes, sir." She smiled in rather pleasant amusement and pointed to a sign he hadn't noticed. "Only we call her a tea-leaf reader. She's at the other end, the big table at the left."

Harry stared and finally located the woman, obviously dressed in some costumer's idea of what gypsies wore, with a heavy shawl and a dark veil over her head. Her back was toward him, but she must have been shaking a cup, from the motions of her arms.

"Would you like her to stop at your table, sir?" the waitress asked.

He nodded, wondering for the hundredth time why New York restaurants couldn't find girls like the ones often serving in such backwater places as this. "How much?"

"Nothing." The girl laughed softly. "We're not allowed to charge for that, though it's customary to leave something on the saucer for her. And you'll have to order the special tea with the leaves. That's a dollar extra."

It figured. Maybe this wasn't such a backwater place, after all. The steak proved to be excellent, and the vegetables were crisp, with no sign of overcooking. Harry enjoyed the meal, including the special desert of the evening that turned out to be apple pie à la mode. Even the coffee was good. He forgot about the so-called gypsy until the waitress came with the pot of tea.

"She's with the party behind you," she told him. "But she won't be much longer, she says."

He nodded. "Is she really supposed to be good?"

"Well . . ." The girl gave a faint shrug. "I guess so. Even if Mrs. Weintraub—she's the owner—complains that she should say nicer things. She's really a very nice girl, though. Not like the last one we had. She drank." She totaled her check and put it beside him. "If that's all, sir . . . I go off now."

He took the hint and paid the stiff total of the bill, together with a rather generous tip. Then he had nothing to do but wait. For want of anything better to kill time, he tasted the tea; he'd expected it to be vile, but the cook must have been English or Irish. It was excellent tea, though a little strong.

And that, he thought, for Grimes! In another few minutes, he'd be consorting over a table with a fortune-teller. It wasn't much defiance, perhaps, but the gesture was supposed to be what counted. The day wasn't entirely wasted.

Once he heard a shriek, quickly suppressed, from the table behind him. The words were too low now for him to understand, but the fortune-teller seemed to be making quite an impression. Even the nasal woman had lowered her voice to something like a whisper.

Then they were breaking up, to the sound of nervous giggles.

Harry was suddenly self-conscious. The room was reasonably full of people now, and he began to realize that having his fortune told here wasn't going to seem a normal masculine thing, somehow. Why it wasn't, he didn't quite know, but he was sure that such would be the reaction. When the girl sat down with him, there'd be a lot of attention focused on his table.

He poured another cup of tea and buried his face in it

51

just as a rustle of cloth told him the girl was taking the seat opposite him.

"You aren't really supposed to drink it, you know," she said. "Not that it matters . . . Harry!"

Ellen Palermo was so heavily made up that he might not have recognized her under the veil, but her voice had given her away and forced him to look up.

She gave him no chance to speak. "Get out of here, Harry! Now! And don't come back!"

"But . . ."

"No! I can't explain, not here. I'll get in touch with you as soon as I can. But now go. Please!"

He nodded and rose, dropping the bill he had ready onto the saucer. But getting out wasn't quite that simple. A large and effortfully smiling woman accosted him to ask if everything was all right.

"Perfect," he assured her. "An excellent dinner."

"And the gypsy? You left so quickly."

He forced himself to smile back at her. "A charming young lady. I only wanted one question answered."

She let him go, her porcelain smile somehow doubtful.

Harry was glad to drop into the seat of his car, but it was several minutes before he started the motor. Well, he hadn't lied to Mrs. Weintraub, or whoever she was. He'd had one question—and it had been answered.

He'd proposed a test of whether he had precognition, based on his ability to locate Ellen. In the most unlikely way and with no intention of coming within miles of this place, he had found her.

He wondered why he now felt like a frightened boy, wanting to hide from the bogeyman under the sheets. And why had he rushed off so quickly at her orders?

He swung the car out of the parking lot and gunned it back toward Manhattan.

# V.

## PARIS

Sid Greenwald had been delighted to leave Germany and try his luck in France. He knew it was prejudice, of course, but he couldn't help thinking of wailing sirens and Dachau the moment he was inside the German borders. Sure, it had been more than a generation ago, and these friendly people had not even been born when the Jews were being sent through the gas ovens. But Sid had grown up to a mounting crisis of horror, and the idea died hard. He couldn't help feeling like a bar of soap when he heard too much German being spoken.

Okay, so they were one of the best friends Israel now had, while the French wouldn't even fulfill prepaid business contracts. But that had been the French government, while the French people were . . .

Now Sid wasn't sure what they were. At least in England and Germany, Sid had received some kind of sensible treatment. They'd looked at his engine, discussed his lab reports, and talked engineering. Here . . .

M. Guerdin raked a rather long fingernail across the picture of the motor. "But not—ah, esthetic, that bulge. You admit that?"

Sid grunted unhappily. The English wasn't bad, though the accent made it hard to follow. "That expansion chamber around the free-piston cylinder is what gives us a higher

53

Carnot efficiency than any other internal-combustion engine," he started to explain. He'd learned enough engineering around Harry to be sure of himself on such matters.

"Ah," M. Guerdin said soulfully. "Carnot. There was a Frenchman. A genius, not? And those injectors. We have fuel injection. To be sure, not on the models for America—your mechanics do not retain it in your adjustment. *Hein?*"

Sid sighed and started again to explain that this injection was so simple and automatic that nothing could go wrong, that the precombustion chamber bored into the piston head was what permitted the use of both low octane gas and a twenty-to-one lean mixture for complete combustion. Now these independent laboratory analyses showed that the pollutant level was far below the minimum of any planned specifications for the future . . .

"Pollution, bah! France has no pollution problem. It's the vines. You should plant grapes—French vines—all over America. Then—no smog!" Guerdin blew out smoke from a vile-smelling French cigarette and smiled with manifest French destiny. "Besides, let us—ah, talk the turkey. To change to your engine, that would cost much money, not?"

"And save a lot more. That's why these plans call for piston drive instead of a turbine. Double-acting pistons, just like those on a steam engine. Used on your front-drive model, you could cut out your differential; one piston would connect directly to each drive shaft. No transmission—the torque holds from stalling right up to full speed, so you don't need to shift, and you can reverse by moving your valves—"

"French drivers," M. Guerdin said in profound admiration of them, "like to shift. It is too bad."

"But all I'm asking is an appointment at your factory with your head engineer. You don't have to approve anything now—"

"Precisely," asserted M. Guerdin, whose auto experience had been gained on camel-back in the former

French Army. "It is too bad. But keep up the—ah, stiff lower lip."

Sid gathered up his papers and figures under the tolerant eye and went out to the reception room, where he could mop his brow in comfort. He was beginning to feel too much what his mirror showed—a man somewhat overweight, tired, and fortyish. Somehow, here in France, he couldn't pretend any longer.

The receptionist grinned frankly at him. "Your lower lip is drooping," she told him, with only the faintest of accents to her English. "Would you like a pin for it, Mr. Greenwald?"

He chuckled as he detected the twinkle in her eyes, and his glance moved from her face—a darned pretty face, he decided—to the intercom on her desk. "You didn't?"

"I heard every word," she assured him. "You never had a chance, you know. I could have told you that, but you haven't been here long enough to believe me."

"When you get off here, try me over a drink," he suggested, but he couldn't get the old spirit into it. Girls had never really gone for him. Of course, he'd heard about French girls, but . . .

"I'm off duty now. I was just waiting to be asked," she told him. "Hello, Sidney. I'm Marie."

"Make it Sid—everyone does," he said automatically. Then her acceptance hit him. "Hey, it's nice to know you, Marie."

It was amazing what could be told over a couple of drinks. All the things he'd meant to tell Guerdin came pouring out; only now they made sense. And she seemed to understand.

"Why not?" she answered his surprised question. "I graduated with very high honors as an engineer. Even my teachers were pleased, though they didn't want me in their classes at first." Then she shrugged. "But as you see, I'm very pretty. So, after they hired me here, they told me I was a receptionist. And you? You know quite a lot, but you're no engineer, Sid. What were you in America?"

"I drove a truck selling ice cream door to door," he admitted. "Until Harry Bronson came along. He's my partner."

She managed to be interested in that. Sid's father had been a machinist, and Sid had inherited his shop. He'd listed it for sale, and Harry had come to look it over. Then somehow, in discussing what he needed, Harry had revealed the whole idea of the motor. Sid, who had grown up in a machine shop and still knew more practical possibilities than Harry, had pointed out changes. In the end, he'd put up for the shop for a half interest, with Harry to provide all other funding—including this trip.

To himself, Sid winced a little at that. All right, so maybe he had padded his expenses a bit. But it wasn't coming from Harry's pocket, exactly. With old Scrooge Grimes holding the purse, a man had to squeeze out what he could get.

"Now tell me why I never had a chance," he suggested, to change the subject.

She laughed. "Your demonstration car when you drove here—it was English. It wasn't French! Guerdin saw it and had to avenge the honor of the Republic!"

Hell, Sid thought, it would be that. They'd cut corners by shipping over just the motor and installing it in England. Maybe he'd better see about getting it switched to a Renault.

"And I suppose you wouldn't get into an English car," he suggested. "Say to go somewhere for dinner."

"You're so slow, you American men!" Marie reached promptly for her purse and was on her feet at once. "I've been dying to try your car. But you must let me drive, of course—after I look at your motor. And I know two nice places to eat. One is expensive and modish. You'd have to let me go to my apartment and wait there with no one to talk to while I change. And you'd be very bored, because I live all alone, and I'm afraid the water for my bath will have to be heated, and . . . But the other place is quite simple and nice."

"Hang the other place and hang the expense. Let's go." Sid did his best to offer her his arm gallantly and was rather surprised when she took it without making him feel uncomfortable.

On the way to her apartment he discovered that she was really French, since she seemed to drive most of the time with her hands off the wheel, like all the other French drivers. He was beginning to understand why French cars had the shortest average turning radius and the best average brakes of any cars in the world.

He learned a lot about Paris that night. And in some ways, the stories he'd read about French girls hadn't been exaggerated.

## VI.

## FREAK

Harry's dreams were troubled, though not with the old nightmare. Something vaguely horrible seemed to be gnawing at his skull, trying to get in to possess his mind. He struggled against it, but his will was sapped by drugs or hypnotism. He tried to cry out—and then found himself sitting upright in bed, covered with sweat. He turned down the heat in the bedroom, and his later sleep was normal enough.

When he woke again, it was morning and the phone was ringing. "All right, Uncle Charles," he answered. "What is it now?"

There was a moment of silence. Then a long, harsh sigh came over the line. "So you've stopped pretending, Henry? All right, you saw Ellen, against my specific orders. I gave you my word, and I'm keeping it. So—your rent is paid for eight more months, and your last allowance check was already sent yesterday. But as of now, you're cut off—cut off completely!"

"You're guessing," Harry told him. "I ditched your spy!"

"Quite true, and I fired him. But I have other sources of information. Good-bye, Henry."

Harry sat up groggily, letting the idea soak in. But it was

too early. He couldn't cope with things until he got some coffee and breakfast. Damn it, Grimes must have had a spy on Ellen. Maybe that was why she chased him off so suddenly. It would be like Grimes, if he hired the service of some agency, to demand complete coverage of all possibilities.

He found that the mail had come and pulled out the envelope that held his check. His allowance had always been more than generous. With the rent paid to the end of his lease and with this money, he might be able to stretch his funds to cover living for a full year—long enough, perhaps, to find some kind of work or for the motor to pay back some of what it had cost. But not if he took care of the urgent request of Sid for more money.

He growled at the coffee that seemed to take forever and began making toast in the broiler. He was in no mood to fiddle with eggs this morning.

Whatever happened, he wasn't going to go crawling back to Grimes to eat humble pie! Anyhow, it might do no good. The old man had read a lot into Harry's inadvertent recognition of the caller's identity before he should have known it. That habit had to be broken!

Funny. Grimes hadn't questioned Harry's ability to make it work. Just what had gone on in that "colony," if it had ever existed? What did Grimes really know and think?

"Insolent young freak," said Grimes' voice suddenly in his head. It was a voice of anger, but there was a feeling of many other emotions—despair, loneliness, and a curious yearning hunger. "I'll see him in hell. And *her!* Oh, damn them, damn the whole lot of freaks!"

The voice either cut off or Harry cut it off. He wanted no more. Such bitterness should never be passed to another.

So he had both precognition and telepathy! He mulled it over and accepted it. There was no doubt in his mind. The abilities apparently worked by fits and starts, however. He wasn't in control of them. And that was bad. It was like a man discovering electricity without understanding. He might use the sparks to start a needed fire, or he might electrocute himself because he didn't know how to regulate the voltage and amperage. Maybe the possession and fear symbols in his mind were subconscious warnings of ignorance and real danger.

Of course, hypnotism might be a control. His first total success had come after Lawson worked him over. But if that was the answer, he had no intention of using it.

Question: What had happened to other people with the abilities? There must have been others to account for the number of stories of psi experiences. It seemed to be somewhat hereditary, like a mutation or group of mutations that must have been building up for several generations. In that case, others must have had anything from faint touches to more ability than he had, probably. What had become of them?

Well, if Grimes' account was true, it had ruined some of them. Something about it seemed to have driven them mad. Also, if the one who'd sent him the note had such powers, the tears he'd felt and the hopeless desperation in her cry would indicate they hadn't done her any good.

Still, for a mutation to survive, it had to offer benefits. He couldn't think of any great value to telepathy, aside from satisfying a sick curiosity, but precognition should have advantages. Why had nobody who discovered those advantages ever made a public announcement or gone to some place like Duke University to prove them conclusively?

His next cup of coffee served him better. He came to the conclusion that such abilities had to deal with information—and that brought them into the field covered by information theory. He'd never paid much attention to that, aside from a cursory study of Claude Shannon's brilliant initial work. It was time he got a little theory to make sense of his few facts.

Dave Hillery answered the phone and had no trouble identifying the mathematician Harry had heard arguing about telepathy at the last Primates meeting. "Sure, Bud Coleman. Wait a minute. By coincidence, he's right here, trying to convince Tina the zodiac is all askew. I'll put him on."

Coleman's voice was pleasantly amused. "Sure I remember you, dear boy. Carnot's rightful place in the history of thermodynamics. You were half drunk but arguing splendidly. And wasn't there something about you in the *Voice*?"

"Yeah," Harry admitted. "That's what started me wondering how psi would fit into information handling. Doesn't it require an impossible bandwidth, or some such?"

Coleman seemed delighted, but he wanted to discuss it all in person. "Put on some lunch, dear boy, and I'll be right up. I've about proved to Tina that the zodiac isn't the same one the Chaldeans knew. Now she needs time to restore the faith and all that."

Coleman was a tall, thin man with a blond mustache and an enormous appetite. He seemed to listen without either slowing his eating or stopping his incessant monologue.

He waved the bandwidth argument aside at once. "Sounds good when I talk to engineers, but not necessary, you know."

True, a signal carrying five thousand bits of information a second required a five kiloherz bandwidth, like that on normal AM radio. That was obviously enough to carry such things as the subvocalized words in another person's mind. But if the signal was to be radiated from the nerve fibers in the brain, it had to be at frequencies in billions of cycles a second—so there would be millions of channels available.

"No problem at all. But not on the spectrum we know." He grinned at Harry's frown. "Excellent pot roast, dear boy. Umm. Normal high-frequency signals can't get through the liquid cushion and bony surrounding of the brain. Besides, we've explored the whole electromagnetic spectrum, so we have to assume a different type of wave for this. No telling what the velocity of propagation would be, either. No reason why it should be limited to our old friend, the speed of light. Couldn't be infinite, of course —or it wouldn't have any frequency or be a wave form. But anything short of that. By the way, Harry, is there anything personal to all this?"

"Why?"

"Just curious. You wouldn't be the first, though. Roommate in college could read my mind. Often got him to bring me books or food that way. Never failed."

"What happened to him?" Harry asked.

"Went to Wall Street, made a killing, and then began brooding. Jumped out of a window one day." Coleman investigated the refrigerator, found some ham, and began making another sandwich. Then he glanced at Harry, and his face sobered. "Oh, dear, it *was* personal! I'm sorry, dear boy. But after all, that's only one example. What name am I thinking?"

"Parsifal," Harry told him absently. Did every case have to end with some kind of insane disaster?

"Very good, Harry. Parsifal it was. You tuned in perfectly."

"All right, what about tuning? How can a man tune into any given individual out of all the millions out there?" Harry asked.

"No problem. Probably doesn't tune in—just a figure of speech. Like FM radio, where a good receiver will pick up one signal and reject another on the same frequency if there's even one decibel difference—twenty percent, that is. Or like listening in a crowd. A microphone can't separate individuals, but you can hear one voice and shut out the others, even though half a dozen are all shouting. A conscious, organic discriminator might be able to handle things with no more than two channels—the same two for all people—like binaural hearing. You have precog, too? My friend did, sometimes. That used to puzzle me until I finally worked it out."

He found the pickles and sat down contentedly, alternately munching on them and sipping his heavily sugared coffee. Harry shuddered and looked away.

Coleman laughed. "Don't mind me. I'm told I have peculiar tastes, though sweet and sour dishes aren't that rare. Oh, yes. Precognition. There is no such thing." He waited for Harry's reaction, and his smile widened. "No, it's true. It's still just telepathy. I'll bet on that. Look, dear boy, we've got a new spectrum of information—we have to have. And since we're assuming that, we might as well go all the way and assume it doesn't act like the old electromagnetic one. It not only propagates in space, but in time—whatever that is. Means the strength of the signal will decrease with the cube of the distance instead of the square, but that doesn't matter. Sensitivity must be in picovolts. Anyhow, the one transmitter most closely attuned to your receiver is your own brain. So you can sometimes read your future mind. Takes care of both powers with one elegant solution. A bit of a paradox, of course. You do something because you did it because you do it . . . Well, closed loops in time are old stuff to science fiction."

Harry nodded. "So you'd only precog things that stuck strongly in your future memory—things you were really interested in?"

"Precisely. Very well put. Ah, beer! I thought I saw it back there. Mind? Of course, I don't believe some of these psychic accounts. Psychokinesis—you know, control of physical objects at a distance by the mind—doesn't figure. The brain would have to do the work, supply the energy. Even if it had enough of that phosphate stuff, it would start putting out waste heat, with no handy sweat glands to cool off. The idiot trying to drive a nail or lift himself by mind power would jolly well soon run a fatal cranial fever."

By the time Coleman suddenly decided it was time for him to leave, Harry's head was swimming and his ears seemed to be ringing.

He had a body of theory now—most of it useless, from a functional viewpoint. Or maybe not—maybe understanding of the possibility of the powers took some of the shock away and at least decreased the chances of the mind losing its normal bearings and drifting into madness. Apparently, that was the major risk.

It was an ugly thought, and one he didn't care to deal with at the moment. In the stories he'd read, all extrasensory powers were lovely wish-dream gifts, adding everything and subtracting nothing. The evil thereof was never mentioned. Life seldom worked that way, however. A man always paid for what he got. But if the price was eventual madness . . .

The word held an amorphous horror for him. It meant the loss of identity to him—but somehow, it meant more, as if it were the key to childhood nightmares. He dropped the thought and turned to more hopeful ideas.

He'd learned one thing, mostly by accident. Picking the name from Coleman's thoughts had been easy—because he'd done it casually, without straining. Now he realized everything had come that way. When he tried to force results, he simply developed a headache. The effort of concentrating somehow closed off the ability. The trick was to relax then, not to force it.

And that was some measure of progress in learning.

He checked his watch and looked up the time for Paris. It would be evening there, which was awkward in a way. But he was somehow sure it wouldn't matter.

This time he was very careful not to strain for answers. He simply lifted the receiver and asked for the dining room of the Hôtel la République, giving its Paris number. It wasn't the hotel where Sid was staying. In fact, he couldn't be sure he'd ever heard of it, though he'd spent several months in Paris once. But he was no longer questioning his abilities.

Fortunately, his French was fluent and his accent good enough to avoid giving offense that would lead to the runaround so quickly used against all non-French barbarians. M. Sidney Greenwald? Would he spell that, please? Ah, yes, the American. Indeed yes, M. Greenwald would be produced but immediately.

The delay was slight. Obviously, there must be only one American, and no paging was necessary. Equally obviously, this was a place that catered only to those with enough money to expect the best of service. Sid must be flying high.

"Harry!" Sid was out of breath, obviously a little intoxicated, and extremely puzzled. "How'd you find me? I didn't know myself I'd be here until an hour ago. What's up? Big trouble?"

"Nothing we can't handle. Grimes has cut us off, but we'll manage," Harry told him. No use putting Sid in a state of uncertainty that would ruin his usefulness or creating puzzles that weren't necessary. He groped for a convenient lie. "Uncle Charles has had you under investigation, it seems. That's how I found out where you were. How are things with you personally?"

Sid's voice sounded doubtful, vaguely apologetic. So he had been living it up on the expense account. "Pretty good, Harry. I'm getting married next week! Wait till you meet her. She's a trained engineer, she'll fit right into the business. But no nibbles on the motor."

"I figured. That's why I called you, Sid. I want you to get back to England at once—be there tomorrow. And see König at the Manchester office."

"I've already seen König. And I'm getting married—"

"Tell Marie she can marry you in England," Harry suggested. It had been an unconscious slip, using her name, but a felicitous one. After that, Sid wouldn't question anything he said. "König's got a hot new engineer and a new investor. He's ripe now."

"Well . . ." Sid began.

A girl's voice broke in. "Sid will be in König's office tomorrow, Mr. Bronson. And I'd love to be married in England. Sid, you tell him."

So Sid also had a new manager, Harry realized. And it sounded as if he'd picked a good one. He was chuckling when Sid assured him there'd be no further delay.

"And Harry—about that money. Forget it. I—well, you know—but I've got a few thousand of my own we can use. Well, what I mean is, we're partners, right?"

"Right, Sid. And kiss the bride for me."

And that, Harry decided as he hung up, was what precognition was good for. He had no doubt in his mind but what König would take an option on the engine and pour in enough research money to get it into commercial production. In three days, Sid would be calling to confirm it.

He had the satisfaction of taking the last trust check and mailing it back to Grimes. Let the old man worry about that. It should at least shake his confidence in his ability to intimidate anyone else.

Harry's power seemed to be taking a nap for the rest of

the day, as if he'd used up whatever energy was involved. Even the phone gave no advance clue when Nettie called again. He stalled her off and went shopping; he'd planned to go anyhow, but Coleman's visit had made it imperative. Then he ate a leisurely dinner, watched a noisy TV spectacular on noise pollution, and refused to think about anything beyond the normal. It wasn't that hard; his mind felt drained and tired, as if some center there had been overtaxed. By the time he went to bed he was generally pleased with himslf.

He was less pleased when he woke up in the middle of the night with his mind filled with the thoughts of a teenage girl being raped by a gang of hoodlums. It faded slowly as consciousness returned, but the horror stayed on. And the worst part was that there wasn't anything he could do. He couldn't call the police; the girl hadn't known the location, but only that it was an old apartment somewhere.

He spent two hours pacing up and down in his living room, trying to shake it off. Enough remained from the experience to sicken him, even then. And the fact that the girl was far from innocent and had provoked the assault didn't help, any more than her violent wish for a knife rather than for help.

Harry had read enough about violence, but he'd been far more insulated from it than he thought. This bore no resemblance to what he'd seen on the television screen. Now he knew the reality of it. And he had a flash of precognition that warned him there would be more. This had been the blow that battered down the door his mind had locked over its telepathic powers. From now on, they would increase steadily.

He still had no idea of how to control them. Apparently he could encourage the powers by relaxing, but once the flash of anything hit him, the most rigid concentration could not turn it off.

There was supposed to be a censor against the mind's own subconscious thoughts, carefully cutting them off when they were too ugly for the conscious part of the mind. What he needed now was a censor against the thoughts of others. But he could find no evidence for it in himself, nor was there any reason why it should have evolved.

It must have taken at least half a million years for man to separate himself from the brute within him, and he obviously still hadn't done a very good job of it. Say two thousand generations of humanity had passed while men developed the censor against the inner beast—and while those lacking the power were pushed back by its absence into lower and lower survival values. If the job was still only half done . . .

The chance for a quick development of a telepathic censor didn't look too bright. Unless the conscious-unconscious censor could take over the job . . .

He spent most of the rest of the night reading through the books on psychology he'd always meant to look at. But they weren't very helpful. No two writers seemed to agree, and there were a number who regarded the whole Freudian concept of a censor or any separation between conscious and unconscious as nonsense.

If he'd had to learn engineering from books as conflicting and vague as that, he'd still probably be thinking that a wheel should be triangular. The mind was the most important mechanism that man had to deal with, but the knowledge about it predated the phlogiston theory.

Nothing the next night was so bad, partly because he'd deliberately worn himself out physically to deaden his senses. But toward morning, vague feelings of distress and violence began to disturb him. He was just awakening when he found his mind linked to a man in the middle of a bad LSD trip.

Harry had never been seduced by drugs. He liked reality generally too well to want to distort it, and he had too much respect for his mind to try inducing any measure of temporary insanity in it. But after even this secondhand experience, he found it impossible to understand how anyone could deliberately risk such a thing. It wasn't the first bad trip the man had had, either; there were memories of even worse experiences.

Abruptly, Harry realized with complete certainty that he would take LSD—more than a single time and always with the intention of causing the most unpleasant reactions!

"Like hell I will," he told himself. He wasn't the type to go that way.

But he *knew* better. And he knew that he was going to have to accept the knowledge now or else give up all his new certainty in precognition. It either worked and he took it for granted, or he'd been a fool to base the whole business with Sid and König on it. He couldn't have it both ways.

In the end, he accepted his flash of precognition, abhorrent as it was, with the reservation that there had to be some good reason for his future behavior. He couldn't precog the reason, but that didn't matter. There had been many things which he had considered horrible while still a child that now were among his pleasures—from eating snails to entertaining girls. Horrible risks then were now pleasant games—and some previous games now seemed dangerous and stupid. He decided that his older self must have more experience than he now had and that he must trust his more mature judgment.

Something seemed to dart toward his mind then in a shocking blow of mockery and laughter. He lifted his hand as if warding off a blow, but it was gone almost instantly, leaving only a vague sense of alien wrongness behind.

That day the telepathic awareness of violence began to increase, even while he was awake. But toward evening he was learning to suppress most of the strength of the emotions by refusing to feel them, much as he could suppress his awareness of boring conversation by mentally closing his ears to it. It gave him his first hope, indicating that he might eventually come to terms with even the violence-polluted mental environment of Manhattan. But it didn't always work.

How could a man walk past a building in which a young father and mother were beating an infant brutally? Harry had known from the news that such things happened and had wondered why they were not immediately reported. Now he knew how hopeless it was; he had no evidence, nor any way to get into the place in time to collect such evidence. Or what could he do about the subtler violence of a mother destroying a girl's love for a man with vicious lies because she also wanted him?

He found to his surprise that the course of wisdom was not to travel in the better neighborhoods, but rather to pick the poorer sections. Somehow, there seemed to be an apathy to the violence he found in poverty that made its impact easier to screen from his thoughts.

When Sid's call came, it confirmed the reality of precognition. König had practically fallen on Sid's shoulders and wept for joy. The man had been searching for him, afraid some other company had already negotiated. Now the option was signed with money due shortly, and it was almost certain that a formal contract would be ready when the engine passed a few simple tests that Harry knew it could take easily. And Sid had a salary as a consultant.

Well, at least Sid was happy.

Harry tried to share the pleasure, but it wasn't what it should have been. He finally climbed into his car and headed out to the shop. Things tended to be rather bad on the highway; apparently, there was something about driving that brought out the brute in most people. But it was at least an inner violence, with little chance for its outward expression. Once at the shop, the level dropped to a bearable background, probably because there were fewer people around and they were further from him, weakening the signals.

He spent the day and night working on various ideas that might yield some kind of screen against whatever it was that served as mental radiation. It was strictly hunt-and-try tinkering, since he had no body of facts and useful theories against which to design. Neither conductors nor nonconductors seemed to help. He collected a small amount of semiconductor material and tried that, but either it was not enough or the stuff was useless—probably useless, he decided.

Putting assorted frequencies and wave forms into a loop around his head worked no better. He hadn't really expected to be able to heterodyne or interfere with thoughts, but the idea had been used enough in science fiction stories

69

to make him try it; sometimes the writers hit on a good idea by accident.

He was tempted to stay away from New York, since that offered some relief. But Ellen had promised to get in touch with him, and her only chance to find him was at his apartment. He finally piled into the Citröen and headed back.

He found a partial answer in his apartment that evening. It came in a bottle marked as a product of Scotland. Alcohol seemed to cut the level of thought down almost directly in proportion to the amount he drank. By the time he was too polluted to take his shoes off before he went to bed, he was as dead to anything psychic or psionic as he'd been during the halcyon days before Lawson hypnotized him.

He paid for it the next day, however. The hangover was bad enough, but the nerve irritation that was left from the alcohol made every message his mind picked up stab through him with at least double the normal intensity.

He took care of that with the hair of the dog, but this time he controlled it, keeping himself to a mild state of inebriation that didn't seriously interefere with his thinking but still cut the impulses down enough so that he could control his reaction to most of them.

Maybe man's ancient craving for alcohol had a reason no one had suspected. All men might have faint traces of telepathic power; there was some evidence in the way mobs reacted with positive feedback, doing things that no individual in the crowd would have condoned. If so, humanity must be awash in a sea of all the ugliness that had been thought of since time began. And those slightly more sensitive must have found the anodyne of alcohol irresistible. Harry wasn't too fond of the theory, but he filed it away for future thought.

He knew that in his own case he was going to have to cut back on drinking shortly. It was a temporary stopgap, at best. The only real solution must come from developing a tolerance to the things that impinged on his mind. And in that, he thought, there was some evidence that he was making progress. A little girl crying over the puppy that had been run over wasn't nearly as bad as it would have been a couple of days before.

It was battle reaction, of course. Men had long experience in learning to live with extreme violence. It was perhaps an ugly adjustment, but one that had been necessary for the survival of the race. Now its ancient strength was working on him. Maybe a man lost something when he overcame his early fear and horror of all painful things; but without the change in values, life would be too horrible to face.

At the end of the week he tried getting along without alcohol. It wasn't pleasant, but he found it possible. And for a time, things began to look up again, except for the fact that Ellen hadn't called.

Now a new phenomenon began, as if there were no end to the tricks his evolving mind could conjure up. He began to have vague bits and snatches of memory about the time before he was ten.

His father remained a formless and faceless person to him, but he seemed to remember talking over some great distance with the man. It wasn't like a telephone conversation, but warmer, more personal. Then there were bits and scenes that apparently involved some little girl he had played with—something about a canceled birthday party, a doll that fell in a creek, and a walk with a very old man who might have been his grandfather. He would have welcomed this beginning of an end to the block to his memories, except that some of the recall was ugly.

His mother remained a void in his memory. But there were sounds of horrible things said in a female voice and replies from what could only be his father. Sometimes those were tired and unhappy, sometimes as ugly as the woman's words. He could never recapture much, it seemed; but he could "hear" his own name a few times, and it wasn't pleasant.

Most of the details were still locked away, and there was no order to what came through. It was as if a few cells in his memory were suddenly discharging accumulated loads, each a tiny segment of memory complete with sound and partial sight—a replay, rather than a normal memory.

Then one bit came through more completely. It was a memory he had seemed to carry with him through his amnesia, though he'd never been sure it was real until now.

He was standing on something—stairs, a rock, or a ladder. And all around him were flame and the greedy sound of fire. Smoke was in his nose, and he was gagging. And over it all came the sound of a woman's voice, alternately ordering him down and crying defiance at something horrible and fearsome but unseen.

*Henry!*

The picture was gone as suddenly as it had come; but his forehead was beaded with cold sweat, and his saliva seemed to pile up thin and bitter in his mouth. He barely made the bathroom in time to be sick convulsively. Even when his stomach was empty, it went on heaving and straining. He collapsed on the floor beside the toilet, letting his forehead rest on the cool tiles there, too weak to move. When a measure of strength returned, it was only to trigger his stomach into more convulsions. He sprawled out again, helpless.

He was vaguely aware that the telephone had been ringing for some time, off and on. With an unclear hope that it might be Ellen, he managed to prop himself up and reach for the instrument beside the tub.

"Mr. Bronson!" It was the voice of the woman who must have sent him the note on the clipping—the voice that had been a faint and desperate cry of despair. "Can I help you? I'm downstairs in your building, but your door is locked."

"Get doorman to use passkey," he mumbled. "Tell him—Joe sent you!"

It was a code he'd let a few of his friends have when they wanted to use his apartment for a meeting during his college days. He hoped the right doorman was on duty.

Then he heard steps in the hall, and he was being lifted from the floor and carried to the bed in the husky arms of the doorman. He brushed off the suggestion of a doctor. "Just drunk, sick hangover," he managed. And it seemed to satisfy the man. He knew it couldn't fool the woman, but he didn't care.

72

She was a queer, birdlike little thing, about thirty years old, with lines on her face no young woman should have. She refused to give her name or talk much, though she stayed through the night nursing him. There wasn't much need for words. There was a flow of something without words from her—a flow in which some hidden anguish was almost concealed by compassion.

She left in the morning, but not before he could ask the one question that was most important. "Do you ever get used to it, miss?"

"For a time," she told him. "And I guess, if you're lucky, you can become resigned. I think my sister did. She was always stronger than I am."

He caught her hand as she reached for her cloak. "I'd like to see you again—under better conditions. Where?"

"You can't," she answered. "Tomorrow—I won't be here. You know how I know that. But it's all right. They won't get me. I just—won't be here. Good-bye, Mr. Bronson."

She kissed him on the forehead then, very softly, and vanished down the hall. And he lay numb with the fleeting glimpse of the certainty in her mind. Tomorrow she would be dead. She was almost happy about it.

There were no more memory incidents during the day. He nursed himself carefully, wondering from time to time at the rest of the picture that lay buried somewhere in his head, horrible enough so that even a small part had sickened him. No wonder he'd blocked the whole off in amnesia. He'd keep it in that limbo, if he could, rather than face what must be lurking back there.

Even the precognition and telepathy functions seemed to have been dulled by his reaction to the memory. Either that, or he was getting used to things. He found he could relax now; the shrieks and horrors of other minds touched him at times, but somehow more distant and less personal.

They stayed at that more distant level during the following week. He wasn't sure whether it was that his mind was growing calloused or that something had come to him from the thoughts of the suffering girl. He didn't yet understand enough about telepathy to know whether it was possible,

73

though she seemed to have imposed some kind of conditioning on him that made him avoid the obituaries. She hadn't wanted him to know her fate fully. He never learned.

She had found the price of her gifts. And whatever it had meant to her, the evil thereof had proved too great.

He was sitting down to breakfast when his own revelation came. He was holding a cup of coffee to his lips, and he barely controlled himself to let the hot liquid spill onto the floor, rather than over his lap. Then he sat frozen in shock.

It came with the total, absolute certainty that was a part of true precognition.

It was the horror he had felt weakly behind the suffering and decision of the girl. It was the thing he had sensed in the mind of the woman who had screamed futile defiance while he stood in the flames of his childhood memory. It was a menace that had touched him faintly in his dreams and been blanked away by his waking mind. Now it loomed as appalling reality, a threat against all the future.

Madness came first. He was going to descend into raging lunacy, as his mother and father had done. There had been no car accident, he knew certainly now. There had been something much worse, in which his own death had been insanely plotted. Now the dark and raging perversions of a mind turning against itself played through him. Beyond that lay only a dark hiatus through which precognition seemed unable to tell him more.

There had been a feeling of further developments, however, and he strained against the barrier, driven by an involuntary need to know. Abruptly, the darkness ahead seemed to clear briefly.

It was no longer his own self he felt, but an alien thing, an entity foreign to all he valued of himself! It was the ultimate evil—a demoniac possession, an alienness struggling to take him over, to dissolve his personality and shunt him aside, to use his body as its puppet. And he was helpless before it! Even now it seemed aware of him and was reaching through his telepathic channels for his mind. He felt motives and values so abnormal to his that he could not

74

comprehend them, though everything in him rejected them savagely.

He wanted to scream, but his mouth was paralyzed in horror. His mind wrenched back and away desperately. Then his connection with the alien entity vanished, though he knew it was somehow still aware of him and waiting.

Three months, his mind told him with the certainty of precognition. He had barely three months before he must pay for his gifts with madness and with a loss of himself that was far worse than any conceivable dissolution of his personality in death or insanity!

## VII.

## DOORS

Ellen Palermo hesitated outside the door to make sure the man was alone inside. She started to knock, then reached out for the knob. As she had known, the door was unlocked, and it opened quietly into the hotel room, now littered with the morning papers. John Cossino sat in the one comfortable chair with his back to her until the door closed. Then he swung around quickly.

"I'm Ellen Palermo, Mr. Cossino," she told him. "And the position is *not* filled, and you owe at least something to my father's daughter."

There was no surprise on his dark, urbane face. He merely nodded. "I guess I expected something like this, Ellen. And I was always Johnny to you in the old days. I left the door unlatched, you know."

"I know, Johnny. And I guess I know it won't do any good. But I have to try."

They billed his act as the best-known proof of "mental telepathy" and loaded the puffs with jargon from Rhine's work now. But it was still the same act she'd read about in the old clippings from her father's notebooks. Cossino had trained under her father during some of the last few years, when he'd been only a delivery boy and her father was the retired king of the mentalists. She'd been a child then, but she could remember.

Now his wife was sick, probably dying slowly, and he had to find a replacement for the act before the next season began.

"All right, Ellen. So I lied to you on the phone. Sure, the position is still open, though I've got a couple of kids who may make it." He sighed, reaching for a cigar and devoting his attention to that as he went on. "That's better than you could do, honey. Oh, I don't mean looks. You have figure enough, and onstage you could be gorgeous. But you haven't got a chance, though it breaks my heart to say it."

Her voice came out tighter than she wanted. It didn't seem right to be begging from Johnny. "I still know the routine. Remember, I used to rehearse it with you for my father. And I've kept up—to keep his memory fresh, I guess. Try me out, Johnny."

"All right." He stood up, gathering his stage presence about him as he moved to the far corner of the room. "Close your eyes, honey. Now. Can you tell me—now concentrate—what I hold in my hand?"

"A wallet," she said. It was a simple test, though the code was buried in the two letters that keyed it. Nothing obvious in the Palermo system. "I see a wallet—a brown wallet."

He went on, and she made the responses automatically, but with the pauses and doubts, the sudden certainties of the act still on tap. He called again, taking her off guard this time.

"Pearls," she said.

"Pearls, honey," he said. But his face was saddened, and he was shaking his head. "Pearls in my head. But the code didn't say it. There was no code that time. You were doing the real thing—the reason your mother never went into the act, the reason Nick Palermo had to break it up. You're reading minds, not codes. And that won't go."

No, she knew, it would never do. Audiences sensed things. They liked being cleverly fooled, but if they ever saw a slip that made them think their minds really could be read, they'd panic—and that would hurt the act and every other mentalist act. She'd had that explained long ago by her father. But she couldn't quite give up.

"You wouldn't have turned me down once."

He shook his head gently. "No, Ellen. And I'm just as grateful now. But I'm not a kid anymore; I know it wouldn't be kind." He sighed. "If you'd been like the rest of us . . ."

"I didn't think you knew about our abilities, Johnny," she said.

"I knew. I knew from the first few months. It never bothered me. To a green kid like me, what was the difference? Both acts were some kind of magic. Only one I could learn, one I couldn't. Fair enough." He took his seat again, staring at her with troubled eyes. "You used to be an honest kid, Ellen. I figure you wouldn't cheat me unless things were pretty bad. You tap city?"

She shook her head. "No, I've still got a little money. I don't want a loan—just a job I can hold."

In the end, she told him the story of her attempt to find her own security. The last job had been her second as a gypsy in a tearoom. And it hadn't worked out. The customers had been delighted at first. Then some got a bit worried—which meant they didn't return. Toward the end she'd even tried to play it safe, but somehow things kept turning up. So she'd been fired, and now the agency was wise and wouldn't send her out.

"Besides," she had to add in her own defense, "Uncle Charley didn't help. Mrs. Weintraub got edgy when his spies came around asking her questions. She thought I must be some kind of Communist wanted by the FBI."

Cossino mashed out a cigar. "Yeah, it never works out trying to fake a fake. And I guess old Grimes hasn't changed much. He used to hate everyone—except me. He kind of helped me get started, you know. So what do you do now, honey?"

"Go back and eat crow. What else?"

"Yeah, maybe that's best." He stood up, holding out his hand. Then he grabbed her and hugged her. "But, in God's love, keep in touch, honey. Don't forget Johnny again."

She found a cab at the corner by chance and took it, giving the old address.

So it was ended. She'd spent more than ten years hiding and pretending, holding in everything that was inside her while her power slowly grew, until it could be held no longer. Then the final shock that left her unable to make believe any longer.

Uncle Charley had suffered, too, trying to pretend along with her. Maybe that's why he had been so savage about the past and what was ahead for her. But she couldn't consent to his plans to save her. She wanted no such retreat or treatment. So she'd tried leaving him, to make it on her own. And now she was crawling back, as he'd sworn she would.

Maybe he'd make a compromise now. She was more than ready to meet him halfway. And maybe it no longer mattered so much to her. She'd given up too much already. A little more might not be that important.

It wouldn't be for much longer, anyhow. And when she could fight to preserve herself no longer, perhaps it would help to have someone near who had at least some knowledge.

She got out, hesitating before the elevators. There was the one that led to the apartment she had shared so long with Grimes, and she still had the key to that in her pocket. There were the other two that led to Harry's place.

She was torn, partly because of her promise to get in touch with him, even though she'd never meant to keep it. But after the one move toward what she thought of as Harry's elevator, she pulled back.

She'd made up her mind years before when she first realized how much she was attracted to him that she couldn't let him hurt himself with her. Maybe there was risk for him, too—but in her case, it was known certainty.

She drew back and turned resolutely toward the private elevator, the key out and in her hand. Then she froze, while her face blanched into a mask of shock.

"No," she whispered. "No. Harry, no!"

She stood beating against the two elevators until one

door opened. There was someone getting off, but she dashed under a load of packages and was jabbing the button to close the door before the man could do more than gasp angrily.

Then she was at the door of Harry's apartment, screaming at him in her mind.

## VIII.

## TWO

The cup slipped out of Harry's hand to crash onto the floor, where his staring eyes saw the pieces scatter through the brown stain of the coffee. He'd have to clean that up, he thought. He liked a neat kitchen. His arm slipped down until it hung limply at his side, with his hand making a small pendulum arc. And then gradually his whole body began to bend forward.

It was all very interesting, like watching the description he'd read of a case of catatonic reaction. Next he'd start to bring his knees up into a fetal position, maybe. No, that wasn't happening. His legs were as limp as the rest of him. He seemed to be slipping down to the edge of the chair now.

This was all wrong, of course. He was supposed to lose control of himself in three months, not now. He had pre-cognition—a very fine case of it, complete with bumps and running sores of the mind. He couldn't fight precognition by collapsing now. That would be cheating. But what was three months, anyhow?

He heard a scream in his mind, and there was a pounding on his door. It was for him, he supposed. Somebody wanted to see him. Did he want to see somebody? He considered the question gravely. Yeah, he had wanted to see Ellen. But that was all right, he had seen her. And she hadn't wanted to see him.

"Ellen?" he asked aloud.

"Yes, Harry. Harry! Let me in. You can't stay alone with that! Not when I'm right here."

"Go away, Ellen. I'll get in touch with you later."

"Harry, please. You can come to the door. Just try it. Please, Harry!"

Funny how clear it was, just like real conversation. Better. He could look through her eyes, could see the number on the door. Never really had vision that sharp through other eyes before. Things always looked different through a girl's eyes. They didn't see curves and straight lines the same. Thought they did, though. They still called them the same names.

"You're a coward, Harry," the voice in his head went on. "Go on, I dare you to try to stand up. I dare you, I double dare you!"

"I never take a dare," he answered seriously.

Something was wrong there. That was a memory that he hadn't recovered—and yet it fitted in with all the other bits and pieces. There'd been the girl and a little brook. He'd gotten all wet, too. Very carefully, he put it out of his mind. He'd had all the memories he wanted. They made him sick, and he didn't want to be sick now.

Funny, he didn't remember sitting on the floor. His tail-bone hurt, too, as if he'd fallen. Maybe he had fallen. A fallen freak? And the creatures of hell saw the sons of Earth, that they were fair play. No, that wasn't right; the quotation was all wrong. Unless it came from a story. Maybe the author meant it to be wrong. That made it all right. And right was wrong and wrong was right.

Regression. That what he was in. He was just regressing. He was going to run away, all the way back to where he came in maybe, and then nothing could catch him. He'd fool them all.

He looked idly at his leg, wondering why it felt wet. Wasn't near the coffee. Shouldn't be wet. Ah!

Yes, it was regression. His bladder was already regressed. He'd heard about things like that. He'd have to tell Ellen about it. He didn't have to take the dare now.

Didn't need to fall in the creek. He was wet already.

"Ellen?" he called out. But there was no answer. Didn't matter. He would soon be too young for girls. Might try playing doctor again, though. I'll show you if you'll show me. That was a nice game, but it hadn't been fun to be whipped for it.

"That," he explained to his wet leg, "is where all the trouble starts. Bunch of grown-ups come along just when things are fun and whip us. Makes us get sex and pain all mixed up. Turns us into masochists and sadists. Must be how all the perversions begin."

He considered his shoes. He'd been able to tie his own shoelaces. But there were no laces. Didn't matter. They came off. And his pants were wet. They came off next. The briefs were more trouble. He had to lift himself for that. But the shirt was better. The buttons just flew off when he pulled hard enough.

He lay on the wet floor, experimenting. By kicking against the stove with one foot, he could make himself slide a few inches. Then he could get his toes underneath and slide back. But he needed more wetness. He tried to provide it, but nothing happened.

It was then he made the discovery of himself. Army doctor had wanted to circumcise him. He was glad he'd refused. Much nicer this way, with the skin loose so it could slip back and forth. It felt good.

He heard the door open and stopped guiltily. He knew what happened when he was caught at that. The woman he couldn't see would beat him and talk about sin.

"Don't," he begged. "Don't whip me. I won't do it again."

But it was only Ellen, tossing the passkey onto the sink counter. She must be cold. She was shivering all over, though she didn't have goose bumps.

"You won't whip me, will you, Ellen?"

"No, Harry. Nobody will whip you." She seemed to want to go on clinging to the edge of the stupid old sink, and her smile was all twisty. Her face was a funny color, too, and her eyes sort of slipped aside every time she

83

looked at him. But her words were warm in his head, mostly. "You can keep on doing it if it makes you feel better."

"Bigger. See?"

She looked away then for a second. "Yes, I see. But that floor is messy, and you'll cut yourself on the broken china. Why don't we go into the bathroom and let me fill the tub? It will be even nicer there."

That, he conceded, was a *good* idea. He'd try it underwater. He should have thought of that himself. He'd never been good at such ideas, though. Ellen had always been quicker at it than he was. That's probably why the woman he couldn't see had called her that nasty little girl. But she wasn't really nasty. He'd bitten her hard once, and she hadn't tasted nasty at all.

"She was a nasty little girl, all the same," Ellen told him. "And she grew up even worse—into a nasty-nice woman. She turned into a rotten prude. Harry, I'm sorry. I'm sorry. I can't—"

She was gone then. But he could hear her turning the water on in the tub, so it was going to be all right. Maybe she had a plastic duck. No, that was all wrong. He hadn't regressed that far, not yet. But he'd bet he could, if he wanted to try. He could probably regress all the way back. Only then he wouldn't have much fun, because he'd be too young.

Ellen came back with a big towel which she threw over him. But it tickled, and he tossed it aside, where it began soaking up the liquid on the floor.

She wasn't shivering so much, at least. Now she knelt down beside him, taking his shoulders. "Harry, I'm not strong enough to lift you. I'll help you up, but you've got to try. Please, Harry, we've got to get you to the bathroom."

"I will if you'll take me by the handle," he told her.

He thought for a second that she was going to whip him, after all. Her face was that funny color again, too, and she was making a harsh sound between her teeth. But she nodded. "All right, Harry. I'll try."

His head felt strange as he got to his knees, and his legs were all wobbly when he stood on them. "I guess I'm a little bit sick," he decided. "I'm all weak, Ellen."

She shook her head firmly. "No, Harry. It only seems that way. You're very strong. Nobody else could take all the things that have been done to you. Even having to go through fifteen years of experience in a month. Oh, I could kill them!"

"Killing's a sin—I think," he said thoughtfully. "Ouch, you're squeezing too tight!"

She made a funny noise, but her arm around his shoulder felt good as she led him toward the bathroom. There he had trouble getting into the tub. But once the pleasant buoyance of the water accepted his body, he felt better.

"You're all over dirty, too," he noticed. "You need a bath now."

"I'll take one later," she promised.

"No. Now!"

Why should that make her cry? She hadn't even cried when he bit her, though she'd been awful mad at him. He started to sniffle sympathetically. "I didn't mean anything, Ellen. Honest, I didn't mean to hurt you."

"No, darling. I know you didn't. It's all my fault. I listened to the wrong people and let myself grow up wrong. And then it was too late. At least, I thought it was." She found the tissues and dabbed at her eyes. Her shoulders gradually straightened, and she smiled at him. It was a good smile this time. "Do you really want me there with you? All right, then."

Girls, he decided, were funny. She hadn't taken her clothes off yet, and already she was starting to shiver again. He never shivered, even in his cold bedroom in winter, until after he was undressed. Boys must be a lot smarter about such things than girls. And why should she turn her back when she took off her clothes? That was silly. She was just as naked on both sides. He wondered what she was thinking of  . .

Now that was funny. He'd known how to find out about such things. Just a little while ago, he had heard what she was thinking. There was—

She turned back to face him suddenly. "No, Harry! Don't even try to remember that. Oh, God, give him time!

Don't make him face it all yet! Harry!"

"Yes, Ellen?"

"Harry, remember—remember when we played doctor under the porch. And I had to take off all my clothes so you could examine me. Remember?"

"You said the stethoscope was too cold," he agreed doubtfully. "And I got whipped. I remember."

"There's nobody to whip us now, Harry. We can play any game we want to. See, I won't whip you. And you won't whip me. And there's nobody else. You can even—even touch me."

He did and she screamed.

He cringed back and started to tell her he was sorry if he'd hurt her. But then she was in the tub with him, and she had his head in her hands and was crying again, hugging him close to her. Girls didn't make much sense. But it felt good. She was a lot more interesting now than she had been under the porch. There were more things to see.

"I won't do anything you don't want," he told her. "I like you, Ellen."

"And I love you, darling. Really." She drew her face back, and it was all streaked, but now she was laughing a little. Then it grew sober again. "And, Harry, you can do anything you want. Anything. Don't mind how I act. I'm just silly. I guess that's because I'm a girl. I know better, but I can't help myself. I'll learn, though."

He reached out a doubtful finger, and she seemed to sitffen; but there was no scream this time. Then he pointed to himself. "I've got them, too. See. Only mine are all little."

"I know." She touched him on the breast lightly, and he giggled. "I can't help it, Harry, being bigger than you are. That's the way girls are when they grow up."

But he'd lost interest by then. He was studying her toes where he could see them beside him. They were so thin, and they bent inward. It must be those tight shoes girls wore.

"I could read minds once," he assured her.

"You'll be able to again."

"No, I mean a long time ago. I could talk to my father
86

when he was far away. I was precocious."

"You told me so then, but I didn't believe you. I couldn't do it until I was fourteen, and then it began very slowly. You must have been very bright, Harry. Do you remember your father?"

He tried, but nothing would come. There was just a vague body without a face and a feeling of something warm and strong in his head. "No. Ellen, were you really truly the little girl I used to play with?"

"Really, truly, darling." She gasped and grabbed the edge of the tub as he explored her body with his big toe, but it didn't seem to bother her as much this time.

The water was growing colder then, and he was glad when she suggested that they'd had enough. She helped him dry off when he was still unsteady on his feet, and let him use the towel on her back. He watched the water running out of the tub.

"Bet I can do something you can't," he challenged her. But he wasn't as good at it as he remembered he'd once been. Even forcing himself, he couldn't seem to urinate for a greater distance than three feet back from the tub. He gave up in disgust. "Better not put those clothes back on. They're all dirty. You can wear some of my pajamas."

He'd expected her to make a fuss about wearing boy's things, but this time she seemed to like the idea. She brought back another pair from the bedroom for him.

"You wait here, Harry. I've still got to clean up the kitchen."

He nodded, trying to remember something. Then he had it. "That's why I couldn't do better. I already went on the floor there."

"I noticed," she admitted. But she didn't seem angry about it. She was a nice girl. Besides, she felt soft and good when she'd let him pull her against him.

The kitchen was clean, and he was a little steadier by the time he followed her out. Ellen had found things in the refrigerator and was putting pots and a skillet on the stove. She said something about an omelet, and he nodded. He'd been taught to eat what was put before him and not to ask questions.

"Don't go away again, Ellen," he asked her as she began to dish the food out onto plates. "I like you here."

"All right, darling. I like me here, too."

He was eating, but he wasn't much aware of what the food tasted like. Something was happening in his mind, and it was more interesting. He was growing up. It had begun right after the bath. The regression was moving into full reverse. And with the change came a wave of embarrassment for what he'd said and done in front of her. He saw her studying him and realized she must be reading his mind. But he skittered away from that, holding to the new seriousness that had replaced his earlier play mood.

"Why have I forgotten so much, Ellen?" he asked.

She was still studying him thoughtfully as he waited for her answer. There was a frown on her face as she thought about something. Then she sighed.

"All right, I'll try to answer some of it. How old are you now, Harry?"

The answer came without his thinking. "Twelve, I guess."

"Yes, that's old enough. You know about what happened to my father and mother—yes, I see, Uncle Charley told you that. She begged my father to do what he did, I think. I wasn't there, Harry. I was spared that. I was somewhere playing with you. And right afterwards, Uncle Charley took me away to New York. I was eight then. So I don't know too much, except what I heard from him and later. Do you know about your own parents?"

He nodded doubtfully. "They told me it was an auto accident. But I don't believe that now. It was worse. She tried to kill me in a fire. Tell me."

"Your father was a very famous surgeon, being called into consultation everywhere. I remember him as almost a stranger and the only man with a beard I'd seen until then. Your mother and he were first cousins. I think she felt their marriage was a sin. Before, she had been my father's partner—but you know that."

"She went insane," Harry said. And something dreadful rose in the back of his mind. But almost at once, Ellen was behind him, pulling and turning his head against her breast.

"Don't, Harry. Not yet. You're still twelve. You'll have time enough later."

"You're very good to me." The dark cloud was receding, though he knew it must return. He went back to the story. "She went insane, and she wanted to kill me. Isn't that true?"

"Yes, Harry. When your father was away, about two months after what happened to my parents, she set fire to the house, holding you inside with her. But your father knew. He came back in time to get her and you both out. Nobody could understand how he did it. But she never recovered. They took her away."

"And my father took me away?"

"I think so. Some small private hospital where they treated your burns. And—I don't know much about this, but I gather he tried something on you. Something mixed up with drugs and hypnosis. And if you and he could really read minds—yes, I see you could—well, I suppose he could reach you directly. He blocked out your memories and your abilities. He meant to save you, Harry."

"What happened to him?" Harry asked. He was feeling some stirring of memory now, filling in the gaps. There'd been a partial block from the shock of his mother's treatment of him. His father had only channeled and deepened it.

"He told Uncle Charley he was going away to have himself confined to an institution. He was partly psychotic by then, too—though who could blame him?"

It made a fuller picture of the past in his mind—enough for him to stop probing further. He had enough to think about. "And then came all the psychiatrists. I can remember some of them. Always probing and asking the same stupid questions. They wouldn't let me mix with the other boys at the school, you know. They were a little afraid of what they called my delicate balance, my potential instability. They thought they were hiding their ideas behind their big words. But I was a doctor's son! They'd have done better to let me alone. I told Uncle Charles so, but he never would listen."

"Sometimes he did," she said. "He listened to me at

89

first. He wanted to adopt me legally, but I wanted to stay my father's daughter. And he never forced me to change that. He wanted to be good to us, Harry. He's a very honest person, really. But he had his problems, too. And then, when I turned fourteen—"

She got up and began scraping the dishes into the sink, getting ready to wash them in the old-fashioned way. "That's when I found I could sometimes read other people's thoughts," she said with her back to him. "That doesn't bother you now, does it?"

He made no answer. If she could read his mind, he didn't have to answer. And she turned her face toward him briefly to smile at that.

"It came on very slowly. At first, just a hint now and then. But I knew it could happen, from your parents and mine, so it wasn't any shock. Until I got all the nasty things. Men and women thinking—ugh! Oh, I knew about sex and such things; your mother had several long talks with me about that and sin, though my mother never mentioned the subject. But I asked Uncle Charley about something I didn't even know was bad, and that's when he found out. He—I guess he was scared for me. He really lectured me then, and he made me promise to give up telepathy. As if anyone could! But he wanted to be fooled, so he was."

She'd been rubbing the same plate for most of her speech. Now she rinsed it and turned to another.

"I got all twisted around inside, knowing things I couldn't understand. But it wasn't too bad, once I learned to shut out some of the worst things. It was very nice in school when we had a test. I could always find someone who knew the answer."

"That's cheating," he protested. Then he winced as her smile indicated he was being very young.

"Of course, but it all seemed natural to me, and I did study my lessons. Besides, the things I learned that way stuck better than the others. I hid it from Uncle Charley, and it seemed so natural I mostly didn't think of it. I wasn't much good at predicting, but I learned to read almost any mind. I thought it was good—until a few months ago."

"What happened then?"

"I learned something horrible, Harry. Something too horrible to tell to a twelve-year-old!"

"I think I know something like that, too. And I'm going to have to go back all the way, I guess."

She nodded, and the dishes no longer gave her an excuse not to face him. "I know, darling. But not yet, please. Stay where you are for just a little longer. You need that—and so do I. Let me be—oh, an older sister for just a while longer, until I try what I have to do."

"You don't look happy about it."

"I'm not, Harry." But she smiled again and brushed the hair back from his forehead. "Yet I'd be much more unhappy if I let you grow up to what you have to face any other way. Really." Then she braced her shoulders and motioned him out of the chair. "Bedtime, Harry."

"But it's still light outside!"

"I know, but you've had a very hard day. And it will be easier if you lie down and relax. Please?"

He followed her, conscious that something was wrong. Then he had it as he watched her making up the bed. "I guess I'd better sleep on the couch," he decided. "You can take the bed."

There was something very tender in the smile she gave him. But she shook her head. She turned back the covers carefully and patted the right side. "You'll sleep here, Harry. And I'll sleep on the left. It has to be that way. Yes, I'm very sure."

This time she didn't turn her back as she dropped the pajamas to the floor. He hesitated, uncertain what to do. His eyes wanted to search out her body, but he was afraid to let her see him look. And his fingers reached for his own buttons, then fell away. But he caught her nod and reluctantly undressed, conscious that he was turning red all over. She waited until he was between the sheets before she closed the blinds tightly. He felt her slide in beside him. Her breath caught just slightly, and then she was pressed up against him.

"How old are you now, Harry?"

He was surprised at his own immediate answer. "Fourteen."

"Fourteen is a very good age," she assured him. "It's a very sweet age for a boy, I think. At least for some boys, from the thoughts I've read. And you're a very nice boy, Harry."

"You don't want to do this," he protested as he felt her trembling in the uncertain arm he put around her.

"No." Her voice was completely honest. "Part of me is sick inside. And yet, I do—for a number of reasons."

She kissed him then, her lips tense as were his, and then softening as if guiding him. "So many other experiences," she said softly. "But it's different when it's myself. I know so much—and so little."

Her arms were soft around him, quiet and comforting. He lay there, desperately wanting to do many things, unable to make any advance. It was her hand that took his and guided it. He felt her tense, but there was no sound from her. And then she was relaxed again.

"You won't be alone, Harry. You won't be alone for a second while you grow back. You'll be part of me, and I'll be in your mind, even before you can be in mine again. Body and mind, Harry. Never alone in any way."

She drew him to her, guided him, until his own body took over and he could force his way with her. He heard her moan, this time in pain, but her arms forced him steadily down. And now her thoughts were trickling into his mind. They were wild thoughts, shifting from moment to moment, from sick disgust and loathing of self to a warmth that enfolded him as completely as her body was enfolding his.

Abruptly, his memory was fully back, with its sick waves of horror and fear for what must surely come. But this time it seemed less strong, and there was another mind with his, a voice in his thoughts telling him it wasn't real, it couldn't be real, that the only reality was here and now.

He had frozen into immobility, but now he felt her move beneath him, forcing a physical response from him at some effort he could only appreciate vaguely. And then there was a sudden surge of triumph in her thoughts, and no effort as she held and responded to him.

The horror of the future was washed thin by the physical

reaction as he finally pulled himself away, drained of energy to think. The states of childhood that he had sought to protect himself were also gone, though the memory of their events remained.

Her thoughts reached him again—guarded and channeled, but with the love too real to leave room for doubt. "Sleep, darling. Don't think anymore, my love."

His mind was already falling through the lethargy toward sleep, and her thoughts crooned a soft lullaby to him. He tried to kiss her, felt her move to take his lips, and then relaxed into complete dreamlessness where there were no visions.

It was still and dark when he awoke. His mind groped for the events that had piled together and then came into focus. The vision of doom was there but still held off. And he could feel Ellen's hips where his arm lay across her.

He groped for her thoughts, but found nothing—only a complete blank. Yet something had awakened him. He tried to remember if he'd sensed any sleeping mind. It didn't matter. It couldn't be that absolute a negation.

With a muttered grunt, he turned over and began quieting his mind, hiding and holding back the word shapes that tried to slide across it, letting only a vague picture of a boy and a girl beside a creek cross his consciousness. Beside him, her body stirred slightly, as if she'd turned her head. But he kept the expressed thought back in the dark cell at the rear of his self and tried to breathe like a sleeping man.

The bed trembled faintly, and there was the softest sound of a sniff.

His hand found the chain on the lamp, and he pulled it as he swung to face her. She was huddled into the sheet, with her arms over her head, but he pried them gently away until he could see her face. Her eyes were red and swollen, and her face was marred by the track of many tears.

"Open your mind," he ordered.

She shook her head quickly, trying to hide her face again.

"Open it, or I'll come in and force it open," he threatened. He had no idea of whether that could be done, and the concept was against every ethic within him; but he tried not to let her sense that. "Open it and you can keep a guard on your thoughts. But if I force my way in, you'll have to let me take what I want."

"You could do it," she decided. "Yes, I think you're strong enough. All right, Harry."

Much of her consciousness was still guarded, but he saw what he wanted to know.

"Was I really that horrible to you?" he asked in shock.

She cried out in protest. "Not you. Never you, Harry! Me! I responded to you—fully, totally. And—but that's what is horrible. I'm as filthy now as all those others. I'm no different. I'm an *animal!*"

"It's better than being a vegetable," he pointed out. "I suppose that if you'd hated every moment, but done it all as pure duty to me, it would have been sinless and beautiful?"

She nodded, her thoughts trying to meet his and make her meaning plain to him. But there was no common meeting ground. Damn it, at the end she had wanted him and had met his passion fully with her own. That, when shared in love, was what he'd been conditioned to think was the highest ideal of mature relationship. There was no lack of love, either.

"We're going to have a helluva marriage while it lasts," he decided wryly.

That brought her upright, so surprised that she didn't even notice his eyes resting on her body in frank enjoyment. "You can't marry me—not ever, Harry!" she protested.

"Normally, I couldn't ask it now. But I've had a fair sample of the kind of courage you have, Ellen. I think it's more than enough to risk what is going to happen to me. And for three months—well, I can let you alone. I'm not wholly a ravening beast."

"Not that. None of that," she said. Then she sighed. "My guard is all down, Harry."

He went into her mind gently this time, until he hit the knot of horror and fear she had held back from him. Then he broke contact, holding his head in his hands.

The shape of her madness and the time of its arrival

94

were almost the same as it would be for him. Three months—and then certain and terrible insanity. But beyond that, her mind grew dark and unreadable; there was a faint sense of some terrible danger, but it was not defined into full alien possession. There was only something—waiting . . .

Maybe, as she had said, her precognition was weak, unable to pierce beyond the shock of her madness. Or maybe, as she had assumed when she caught the shadow of his horror earlier, his Alien Entity was only a further paranoiac delusion from his own mind. But he could not accept the idea. That alien presence could be no projection of his own imagination. It was sane—horribly, grotesquely sane in a way no normal human mind could match.

He tried to conceal the direction of his thoughts from her now and to pretend acceptance of her explanation, however. "How long have you known, Ellen?"

"Fully? Several months. That's why I couldn't pretend any longer to Uncle Charley. But the knowledge has been growing in me for three or four years. It didn't come all at once, like yours. I had time to get used to it."

"Does everyone with extrasensory powers have to go mad?"

"Uncle Charley couldn't find anyone who escaped it in the original group. All went mad, Harry."

He pulled her to him, and there was no shrinking this time as she sought his comfort and strove to give him hers. "Then we'll go mad together," he decided. "The time is the same for both of us, so far as I can tell, and even the delusions of our two dooms match, mostly. Could such similarity come about unless we share our lives from now on?"

She considered it, then shook her head against his bare breast. "But there isn't time for me to change, to learn. I couldn't promise to be a real wife to you. And we—we could never dare to have children."

"No," he agreed firmly. "But stay with me. There's room here for whatever arrangement you want. Or I can get a sofa-bed for the living room. Don't leave me, Ellen."

She nestled closer to him. "I already promised that,

darling, or don't you remember? I promised it to you when you were only a little boy lying on a very dirty floor."

"A pretty horrible little boy, as I remember."

"Yes," she admitted. "And I was once a nasty little girl, wasn't I? I really led you astray then. What happened to me?"

"We were brought up by what passes for adults in this world!"

They were silent then, while he rocked her gently back and forth, feeling the softness of her skin slide against his.

"Grimes will have to know. He won't like it, but he's entitled to know we're together. And that means you'll have to make it legal, Ellen—whatever you do in your heart. So tomorrow we apply for blood tests and then get a license. And after that, I've got to start finding some way to get us out of this. After all, we don't *know* what happens beyond that moment—or eon, whatever it is—of madness. Even my hints don't prove any outcome. I've got to try to learn. We've got three months. Sometimes a lot can be done in that time when it has to be."

He sensed a casual consent in her mind, but no hope. And he knew that he was really only whistling against the wind. But he couldn't sit back supinely and let things just happen. A man had to fight for his fate, even when there was no seeming chance to win.

"Only three months," she muttered.

She bent her head back and pulled him down suddenly, her lips seeking his. There was still a sickness coiled inside her, but she met it and drove it back with no flinching from his awareness. There was love in her mind and growing passion in her body.

His own fusion in mind and body met her divided response, accepted it for what it was, and poured out to envelop her as her body received him.

# IX.

## HOME

Dr. Byron Coleman, FRS etc., glanced one more time around the room that had been his home so long. He checked the drawers in the rickety little dresser, looked in the closet, and opened the medicine cabinet above the rust-stained sink. There was only the old-fashioned straight razor, and he tossed it into the wastebasket; almost certainly, they wouldn't let him keep that where he was going.

"That's it, Pete. I'll take the other bag." He picked it up and took the notebook from the scarred table, to follow the old desk clerk down the frayed carpet of the hall and the stairs. Outside, the limousine was drawn up to the curb with the liveried chauffeur beside it.

Pete lifted the bags into the trunk, but waved aside the bill he was offered. "I hate to see you leave, Bud," he said. "After fourteen years, we're going to miss you around here."

"Fourteen years," Bud agreed. "As they say, how time flies. Well, dear chap, take care of yourself."

He shook the gnarled hand gravely, took one more look at the ancient hotel, and climbed into the limousine. "You have the address, James?"

"Yes, Dr. Coleman. My instructions were quite complete."

"Excellent. And by the way, what *is* your name?"

The chauffeur permitted himself a slight smile as he looked back. "It really is James, sir."

The car got into motion with a velvet smoothness, even on the rough streets of the decaying neighborhood. Bud sank back into the luxury of the seat. It was finished, or almost so. By now his books would be delivered to the library of the Primates, his personal things to the friends who could appreciate them. There was a case of good whiskey being sent to Pete, and only the notebook with its charts and graphs, its facts and questions, remained. Then a leisurely drive southward and an excellent dinner at the Canvasback Inn in Delaware. After that, a ride over mostly rural roads, to arrive in time for a final chat with the director, before he sought his very private quarters and the door closed finally on him. He would even sleep soundly this last night, he knew. *Ave atque vale!*

Like all things worth doing well, it had been expensive to arrange. But now, watching the quiet efficiency of the chauffeur, he was satisfied that there would be no fault, ever, with the service for which he had contracted.

The limousine drew up before the West End apartment and double parked with the assurance only such a car could command. Bud waited for the door to be opened and stepped out, the notebook under his arm.

"I may be awhile in here, James."

"Yes, Dr. Coleman. You'll find me waiting here when you come out."

He could have delivered the notebook before, once he was sure the boy had rediscovered his abilities, but now he was glad for the delay. He was curious about the new bride Bronson had taken, and Tina Hillery was never a good person to trust for important details. He knew less of Ellen than of most of the mutants he had discovered. Now, as she held the apartment door open and he introduced himself, he was satisfied. Harry had chosen well.

She had changed a great deal in growing up from a saucy little girl in frizzy curls, but he thought he might still have recognized her. For the moment, however, the recognition wasn't mutual, though she did seem a bit puzzled.

She was inviting him in, explaining that Harry should be

back soon. "Can I give you some lunch, Dr. Coleman?"

"Please, my dear—just Bud," he corrected her. He laughed quietly. "Ah, yes, I see that Harry has told you of my appetite. But no, dear girl, no lunch this time. Not even a bottle of beer. I shan't stay long. Just dropped by to leave Harry my notes about something we're both interested in. I'm leaving town, you see, and I'm afraid I won't be back. Devil of a nuisance, wrapping things for mailing, so I thought I'd bring the book here."

"Thank you. It looks like an awful lot of work," she said uncertainly, but her frown was not directed at the notebook lying on the coffee table between them. "You can't have done all that since talking to Harry."

"Good heavens, no. It took years—most of my adult life, and I'm older than I look. You might say collecting data on all the telepathic mutants I could locate was a bit of an obsession with me. Oh, come, my dear—don't look so surprised. Harry must have let you know I shared his secret."

She shook her head. "It wasn't that. I just remembered you. You were the professor from Yale who came to see Dr. Bronson about your wife. And after she died, you kept coming back. You gave Harry a pocketknife with a green handle for his birthday."

"Did I? Yes, you're right, dear girl, I'd forgotten." He smiled at the memory. "And that's when I began this notebook. I always meant it for Dr. Bronson's son, if he recovered his power."

"But—but you couldn't be! I'd have known at once if you were—were one of us." Unconsciously, she'd drawn further back in the chair, as if trying to reestablish some distance between them.

"Are you quite sure?" he asked. For a moment more, he kept the flow of surface thoughts that served better to guard his mind than any blanking out could have done. Then he began to open some of the memory channels of his thoughts to her. "The human brain has its limits, my dear. But it can learn quite a few tricks when it thinks it must."

His development had been the earliest in his records, even though he was only a second-generation mutant. His wild talents were beginning well before his father was killed in a coal mine disaster and his mother went into a fatal collapse on learning of that. Then there had been the years at the ill-funded and overfilled orphanage. It had been a rugged school for him, teaching conformity to all the ways of the ungifted—even within his own mind. And the long struggle up from his background had deepened and refined his ability to conceal any difference that would not be accepted by the clever minds he had chosen to live with.

He began to close his mind to hers then and to rebuild the pattern that was his shield. But as he did so, he felt her seemingly relaxing probe suddenly sharpen and penetrate, before it withdrew completely.

"Oh, Bud!" She was on her knees in front of him, her hands clutching his tightly. "You can't go there alone! Let Harry and me come with you!"

He freed one hand to brush the hair from her forehead and then lifted her chin until her eyes met the smile that was still on his face. "The doctors will be good to me there, my dear. I've seen to that. And I think nothing—nothing at all—will bother me there. Look again—deeper this time."

He had never felt another mind completely free within his own since his wife had died, and it was something he had missed. He guided her probing thoughts gently, refusing nothing, showing what she might have overlooked. And then he ended it and was alone with himself again.

"You're not afraid," she said wonderingly. "Not at all afraid. You can accept even that!"

"Even that," he echoed. Then he sighed and rose to his feet, helping her to stand beside him. "But now I really must go. You'll see me to the door, of course? And I don't think Harry would mind too much if you were to kiss me once in farewell. After all, dear girl, I did know you long ago."

It had gone rather well, he thought as the elevator took him down.

He settled himself comfortably into the waiting limousine and nodded as the chauffeur resumed his place. Yes, it had gone quite well.

"All right, James," he said. "You can take me home."

# X.

## SEARCH

Harry got up from the kitchen table, stretching his cramped muscles and glancing at the clock. He'd been aware of daylight coming in the window for some time, but hadn't realized the day was that far advanced. He'd been digging into Coleman's notes longer than he'd planned. No wonder he felt stiff. He turned on the heat under the coffee and tiptoed toward the bedroom, where Ellen was sleeping.

She was curled up tightly on her side, but a faint wash of vague sleep images reached him, telling him it was one of her better nights. The past month had been hard on her. Now, however, it seemed she was winning the torturous fight within herself. Somehow, Coleman's brief visit seemed to have given her more strength to face herself as she really was. Her thoughts were jumbled, but peaceful enough. And even in her sleep, she seemed aware of his mind touching hers; she stirred faintly, and something warm and soft reached out gently toward him.

Well, he'd wondered what was the value of telepathy. Now he knew.

The smell of scorching coffee roused him from his reverie and sent him back to the kitchen. Mechanically, he began dumping the pot and cleaning it to make fresh.

The odor of the ruined coffee must have roused Ellen. He heard her going into the bathroom and drew his mind back from her. As part of her fight with herself, she refused to put up a blanking guard even where it would be normal; but the first week of marriage had been time enough in which to establish those areas where privacy was important, and Harry respected them now without conscious thought.

She came out in a brief robe, glanced at the clock in surprise and then at the table where he had been working. Her thoughts were concerned for him and his lack of sleep, but she made no comment. She poured herself a glass of orange juice before she began bustling about to prepare breakfast.

"I heard you come in, but I couldn't get myself up," she said. "You were awfully late—long after the library closed. Oh, Harry! You went to see that Jamieson woman. Was it so horrible?"

"It wasn't good," he admitted. He let her see enough from his mind to give a general picture.

Coleman had discovered and kept records on nearly two hundred mutants, but then had turned to theoretical considerations ten years before, with the result that the larger part of his notes was of little value now beyond a list of names to track down. The Jamieson woman had been seemingly the most hopeful evidence of recovery. She had been institutionalized twice but had made enough progress to be released, and the notes indicated she still had telepathic powers.

Unfortunately, she did have them—though she was no longer consciously aware of them. She had fragmented her mind and blocked them off, though they were all that enabled her to avoid the consequences of her present sick quest for satisfaction in a dulled world. What Harry had found in the back of her thoughts offered no answer to any problem. She was living in terror of something—but the threat was too blurred for him to see whether it was alien or not. Anyhow, he was pretty sure she'd soon be unable to pretend sanity. With the best of luck, she might wind up in some violent ward.

"I told you to leave her to me. Women's minds are easier for a woman. I was going to see her today," Ellen protested as she placed the food on the table.

He salted his eggs and began eating mechanically, shaking his head. "Sure, I should leave them all to you. Honey, I'm no tower of strength like Bud Coleman, and I know I've collapsed every time I've had a real shock. But I'm not quite weak enough to hide behind you every time something has to be done."

"You're *not* weak, darling," she said positively. "I told you that before. Most of us have trouble learning to handle in ten or fifteen years what you've had to learn in a couple of months. Bud didn't think you were weak. He thought you were the only one of all of us who had any chance of finding a solution. But you can't do everything yourself."

"I can't seem to do anything. If I only had a full year—" he began for the hundredth time. But he didn't; he had barely two more months of sanity. One month had already been spent in what he now knew were basically wasted efforts.

"You'd better get some sleep," she suggested. She finished stacking the dishes in the dishwasher, then followed him into the bedroom to begin changing to street clothes.

He watched her, again conscious that she was making progress in her efforts with herself. She was beginning to enjoy the pleasure he felt in looking at her, and there was a hint of the provocative as she reached back for the zipper on her dress. She sensed his approval and smiled. Then she sobered quickly.

"Oh, I forgot. Harry, Uncle Charley called last night. He wants you to see him."

"I don't need his damned money now," Harry told her. For the two months left, he could have made out well enough even without the option money that had finally come through from England. But he sighed and gave in to Ellen's desires. "Oh, all right. I'll see him when I get up."

She kissed him, her mind already worried about handling the agonizingly slow search through the newspaper microfiles at the library. He was vaguely aware later of her pleasure in getting a cab quickly, but he lost her as his thoughts turned back to his problem.

He still had no clue to what he thought of as the Alien Entity. There was no hint of it in Coleman's notes, nor had

103

he found conclusive evidence in any other mind. There was always some lurking menace behind the madness he had seen elsewhere, some fear of terrible change, but nothing definite, in the same way his own vision had been real. He could still recall his horror, though he found it impossible to remember the specifics about it that had created his revulsion.

Somehow, though, it must be related to the madness that seemed the doom of all those he had learned to call mutants. Perhaps the madness was a result of the threat of alien possession—it seemed probable. There were some things no sane mind could bear. And in that case, the retreat into insanity might be a real defense against the possession, making the mind useless to the Alien Entity. On the other hand, it was a possibility that madness was itself a trap, making the mind defenseless against whatever was trying to take it over. He had found no evidence of a mind that had been through its insane phase and was then occupied by any alien presence, but that could mean only that it was too clever for detection.

He had tried to imagine what the Alien menace could be, but there was no way to guess that. Fantasy writers had assumed possession by immortal minds, by creatures from beyond time and space, and almost everything else, including true demons. What he could remember of his precognition made him doubt that the Alien Entity could be anything human, but he had no clue to what it might be.

He had let Ellen's idea that it was only another delusion of his madness stand as if he accepted it, so far as their conversation was concerned. And in a way, he had to treat it so. There was a body of data concerning madness, and he could deal with that to some extent, but nothing on alien minds. Anyhow, since the burst of madness came first, he was forced to look for a way of holding that off. Then, if he could somehow pass through that, he might be able to begin on the further horrors of the later threat. But so far everything looked hopeless.

He sighed in fatigue and tried to drop his worries, building up his guard against obtruding thoughts as he began to fall asleep. He was now able to control most of his powers

104

in ways that had seemed impossible before. There were only background impulses from the mass of human misery around him and a few merely disquieting dreams of his own.

Then he was sitting upright with a scream ringing in his mind and the shriek of subway wheels grinding against brakes, ending suddenly . . .

Miss Jamieson had blown far earlier and more wildly than he had expected. The full awareness of that hit him, together with the realization that his probing might have been what broke the barriers she had built against herself. He fought his adolescent guilt reaction with the honest knowledge that it was almost certainly for the best in her case, but he could win only half a victory from such truth.

The clock said he had been asleep less than three hours, but there was no more rest for him. He stumbled out to the kitchen to reheat the breakfast coffee. It was bitter in his mouth.

The phone rang, and he answered with no effort to conceal his foreknowledge of the caller. "Hello, Uncle Charles. I was just about to come up."

"Oh." There was a slight pause, as if the fairly polite words had taken the old man by surprise. "Henry, can you read my mind from down there?"

"I thought you considered all that pure nonsense!" Harry switched the receiver so he could pick up his coffee with his right hand. Then he decided to answer honestly. "I can. But I don't intend to, unless you force me. What is it you want?"

"Two things. First, to thank you for the invitation to your wedding. Though I don't usually go where I'm not wanted."

"You could have come," Harry told him. It wasn't the most gracious way of putting it, he realized, but habits were hard to break.

Grimes seemed to accept the intent, however. "Ah. Well, I also wanted to give you some good business advice. I can guess why you're trying to find out things about certain people. But you're going at it all wrong. And I don't like your using Ellen to interview them. You can go to hell to your own tune, Henry; but she's a decent girl, and you have no right getting her mixed up in your dirty business."

"And you have no right having her followed. Damn it, she's my wife now!"

"Then treat her like one, not like a paid flunky! No, wait." Grimes stopped to cough before resuming in a more restrained voice. "Henry, I don't want to quarrel with you this time. And I'm not telling you what to do—just how to do it better without involving her. You're both clumsy amateurs. So when you don't know how to do something, you hire an expert who does. That's what private investigators are for. Get one!"

Harry grunted, wanting to kick himself. Grimes was absolutely right! He and Ellen were amateurs, and there wasn't enough time for them to learn how to locate persons and information. He'd been an idiot not to have found trained help from the beginning.

Grimes seemed to misinterpret the delay in replying. "Look for one in the phone book if you don't trust the ones I use. And if you're worried about the cost, have them send the bill to me and I'll pay it."

And that, of course, was his real point, Harry thought. The old man was still being clever. He'd pay—and the man who paid the piper called the tune. With an inside source like that, he could spy on them much better than by using any outside tracers.

"I'll think about it," he conceded, trying to sound unconvinced. "But why should I trust your advice now when I've never been able to get any of the information I need from you before this?"

"Because I'm helping Ellen, not you, you ungrateful whelp! What information?"

"Background facts. For instance, the old man Ellen and I remember playing with in that colony—was he one of our grandparents?"

Grimes snorted. "You must mean my uncle. A worthless bum I had to support, but you kids always liked him. You never acted that way around me. Anyhow, if you want to know about your grandparents, stop being so damned indirect and ask what you want to know. I can't tell you much. Ellen's grandparents were never mentioned. Your father's parents died in a train wreck when young—legitimately, I discovered. But your mother's—well, they went suddenly wild about some cult religion and ran off together, leaving your mother to an aunt—and leaving some pretty wild stories behind. Your mother was very young, but it left scars on her, I'm afraid. I tried to trace them once, but they had simply vanished." His voice had been growing reminiscent, but now it sharpened. "What else?"

"Where's the Idle Hollow Retreat?"

There was an amused bark from the phone. "So you've discovered your mother is still alive, eh? Your information is about fifteen years out of date, Henry. It proves you need an expert. That place went out of business, and I had her transferred. Anyhow, what are you planning? A visit? Don't!"

"Why?"

"All right, see her then! Maybe you should, to see what kind of muddy waters you're fishing in. I'll have the office prepare directions along with a letter authorizing you as her son to see her and get it all delivered to you. Now—what about that agency?"

"I'll hire one," Harry agreed, tacitly accepting the old man's assumption that the information had been given as part of a bargain.

He hung up and began studying Coleman's early notes again. He had realized that the man's real interest lay in building a theory, but had assumed that the early collection of data on telepaths would be more immediately valuable. Now he could no longer trust it. If the brief entry on his mother had been that long out of date, how useful was anything else? His father was listed as having disappeared without trace after being released from a course of shock therapy, but in seventeen years, would he have remained traceless? There was no sign Harry could find that Coleman had ever gone back to the original data to revise or update the entries.

He dug the classified directory out of the closet and turned to private investigators, amazed at the length of the listing. There could no longer be any question of his need for such help. And, fortunately, the option money should permit him to pay for it himself.

How could anyone choose one from among all the listings? The answer came as a sudden flash of precognition, and he turned the page quickly. There was a single line entry for Robert Gordon, with an address much closer than that of most other agencies. A woman's voice with a slight accent answered his call and gave him an appointment within the hour.

The office turned out to be a single room in a ground-floor apartment, with a private door to the hall. There was no lusty secretary, no trench coat over a chair, and no empty liquor bottles and filled automatic pistols strewn around. Nor did the man who shook his hand and waved him to a seat resemble anyone in the private eye films. Robert Gordon was a rather husky, middle-aged Negro of medium height who walked with a slight limp and whose smile was businesslike in a pleasant but undistinguished face.

He leaned back in his chair, studying Harry thoughtfully. Then he nodded. "I thought I recognized your name, Mr. Bronson. You get to remember such things in this business. I used to work for the agency employed by your uncle, Mr. Grimes. Good. I know enough about you so I won't have to waste time making sure you don't want your information for some illegal purpose. That helps."

He went into the matter of the various services offered and his rates with a casual assumption that money meant nothing to Harry—as would have been true at one time. His full-time services were based on a sort of portal-to-portal hourly rate, plus expenses. It wasn't cheap, but the amount he named came to considerably less than Harry had expected.

With that business settled, Gordon took the envelope with the names from Coleman's notes and the other information Harry had accumulated and began going through them, asking an occasional question until he was generally sure of what Harry expected. He nodded.

"Sure, I can take care of most of this, Mr. Bronson. But

for a couple of these neighborhoods, you'd probably get more cooperation by having a white operator do the investigating. You can either arrange that or let me sort of subcontract it."

It probably wouldn't matter, Harry thought. If anything worthwhile developed, he'd want to see about it himself so that he could check directly by telepathic probing.

"You handle the whole thing any way that seems best," he decided gratefully, and saw Gordon's brief smile of satisfaction. "How soon do you think you can have something for me?"

"With any luck, it shouldn't be long." Gordon had been sorting the items into several piles. Now he pointed to the largest one. "That's all pretty much routine—old records and such to check. I usually turn that over to people who specialize in such research; it's faster and cheaper. I'll put several to work at once. You can have their full reports along with a digest and summary from me. Say a couple of days for the first report."

He began asking for more details on just what Harry wanted, some of which were hard to supply without giving away too much. But he seemed to accept even the most obvious evasions with only a slightly amused look. One area of investigation that had been worrying Harry was dismissed with a casual shrug.

"Columbia had a research program on these communes a couple of years ago," Gordon said. "Your answers are probably all in that. I'll get a copy of the final paper and send it along to you with my report."

As he headed home, Harry felt the first relief he'd known since the inevitability of doom had hit him. There was still an incredible amount for him to do in less than two months, of course, but at least the mechanical parts would be taken from him and from Ellen. Now the biggest problem was that he really had no idea of what course he should pursue; so far there had been no hint of a possible cure that left more than a shell of a man after years of shock therapy—and as opposed to that, he could appreciate Bud Coleman's choice of remaining mad.

He sent out a mental shout for Ellen, not expecting any

109

response. He'd tried it before, but the limit of distance he could span deliberately seemed to be less than a mile. This time, however, he received a faint response; she probably hadn't received his full message, but he was aware that she was returning to him, which was all he cared about. He could fill her in as she neared the apartment.

Grimes had kept his word. There was an envelope in his box with a hand-inked map and permission forms to let him into the rest home upstate where his mother had been moved. He memorized the map quickly as he made a fresh pot of coffee, then shoved the papers into his coat pocket.

Coleman's notes still lay on the table, and he turned to them automatically, though he no longer expected much from them. The data were obviously badly out of date, and the elaborate mathematical treatment of Bud's theories offered little hope, however much the work might prove and explain about the history and development of the psi powers among people like him. The years of thought had availed nothing to Bud in the end.

The last half of Coleman's notebook was devoted to his theory—or perhaps only a body of speculation, since there were indications that Bud had not been fully satisfied with his own work. Harry could not evaluate the gene charts and the tracing of potential fractures between the four-letter clumpings of DNA. But the basic idea seemed to make some sense, and it wasn't too complicated.

Sometime near the end of the last century there had been the beginning of another mutation among some of the human race. There was nothing too unusual about that; mutations went on all the time, though most were small and often nonviable. It had been discovered fairly recently that disease and many drugs could produce changes in the germ plasm. But this change had been complex, involving more than one gene and with a number of random shifts. As best Harry could understand it, it seemed to take three generations as a general rule before the result was fully stabilized. The resultant mutation was recessive, but that hadn't mattered; those who had the mutation to any usable degree tended automatically to mate with others in a process of mental like calling to mental like. Those who had

110

any of the extrasensory ability from the mutation either found mates from their own kind or remained unattached. Since Coleman's charts seemed to show that there were certain similar areas of possible mutation in most human hereditary material, it was not surprising that many similar mutations should have been produced by the strong mutagen that produced the original change, so that it should have occurred spontaneously to a fair number of human offspring.

Harry had been surprised at the suggestion of the causative agent. Coleman had traced it to certain volatile hydrocarbons released into the atmosphere from raw petroleum. The time at the end of the last century had seemed wrong for that, since the automobile wasn't in general use early enough. But the encyclopedia confirmed the figures in the notebook. Before the internal-combustion engine, petroleum had been a valuable source of kerosene. Millions of barrels had been distilled, and the lighter and more volatile fractions had been boiled off or burned into the air as waste in the production of fuel for stoves and lamps. The conditions of such distillation had been ideal to produce the hydrocarbons most likely to trigger the mutation.

Actually, the need for gasoline, composed of the more volatile parts of petroleum, had probably decreased the amount of mutagenic agents now in the air. If the mutation was still going on, it might yield less complete results currently; the change had already taken place, and only time could decide whether it would become the norm for the race or be rejected, along with countless other blind alleys in human evolution.

Coleman had speculated on whether telepathy was something mankind had possessed originally in rare and uncontrolled manner, then dismissed it as unprovable now, since the race must be contaminated by countless cases of those who had been born with some of the mutation, but not enough to produce useful results.

It was all a lovely bit of theoretical work, and it might be true. But it had provided no new knowledge on the question of whether there was any way to handle the fact that

111

telepaths—so far as Coleman had discovered—inevitably went mad, and often horribly so. Coleman's notes had yielded no suggestion that the instability might be separated from the basic abilities conferred by the change.

There were a few hints that the aberration had involved a fear of possession in the early accounts. But the later notes gave no weight to that. The work was of no use in that respect.

In many ways, Coleman's theories made the case more hopeless. If the madness were only a reaction to the stress of psi, then it might be treated by relieving that stress by drugs until a final adaptation could be made. But if the instability were inherent, a matter of the basic cell makeup, then there was no answer Harry could see. Science wasn't yet able to reshape the human gene patterns, even in much less complex cases of mental retardation. If the pressures that led to madness were due to the fear of possession or were forced to make possession easier for whatever the Alien Entity might be, then any normal answer was hopeless.

Harry had already decided that his only chance was to treat the madness first, since it had seemed to precede the other menace. If some way through that period could be found, a sane and stable mind might then be able to cope with whatever came later.

There should be some answer. Find one man who has been through it all and had recovered or been cured somehow. With that background and the ability to enter the mind of a distressed mutant, he should be able to guide the aberrant thoughts from madness back gently to sanity. But that was like the instructions for taming a unicorn—first find the unicorn!

So far, the only cures were hopeless. They were apparently either like Miss Jamieson, who could be given a superficial semblance of sanity only at the expense of deeper madness, or they were totally lacking now in any of the psi abilities. Tranquilizing drugs produced only a temporary helpful effect. And the harsh therapies that were capable of aging memories and blasting the madness from the mind seemed inevitably to ruin the apparently delicate

112

mental mechanism of telepathy. The three cured cases Harry had discovered so far were now convinced that their ability had been only a fantasy. They were completely normal in their powers and attitudes—but they were less than normal in their inner selves. Something inside them was lacking, and their minds were vaguely and miserably aware of the lack. Effectively, they were vegetables now, however well they might do on intelligence tests.

Harry wondered briefly what his own father must be like after the long course of shock treatments indicated in Coleman's notes. He shuddered and forced his mind away from the thought. For a second, there had been a vague picture in his mind, but it was gone before he could seize it.

Ellen came in then, asking a few questions only while she probed his memories quickly with his tacit permission.

"Gordon's wife is nice," she said. "Korean, isn't she?"

He frowned, trying to remember. He hadn't consciously noted, but now he could barely remember a small, pleasantly smiling woman who had come in with some typed pages while Gordon was going over Harry's material. Ellen had apparently caught the memories he had and dragged out more details than he was consciously aware of. It was one of the tricks of mental impenetration that he was only slowly growing used to.

Then Ellen nodded and went in to change, accepting his decision to take the trip upstate as she accepted most things. Someday, when her phobias had finally vanished, they would probably have the granddaddy of all battles as she reasserted her equality with him—if they had time enough for that. But until then her mind pictured her as less than a full woman and hence only half human. He led, and she followed. It bothered and distressed him, since he was well aware of the quality of her mind, but he had forced himself to wait patiently, as she forced herself to accept his annoyance with no outward sign.

There was also the factor of Bud Coleman's assessment of Harry's abilities as ones that offered the only hopes for the mutants. Ellen had accepted that, though Harry could see no reason for it. So far he had managed only to fall apart at every emergency within his mind; his contributions to any solution were exactly nothing.

"You don't approve of my visiting my mother," he called out to her. "Why come, then?"

"It'll be a nice drive," she answered. There was the slinky, pleasant feeling of a satin slip sliding over her hips—something no male mind could ever tire of.

It was a nice drive. The weather was almost unseasonably warm, making the day seem like spring. Yet once beyond the city, there was still the white of the last snow on the country. The trees were dusted, their bare branches turned to fairy things in the light of the sun, and the air had a crispness and flavor that could be appreciated readily by anyone used to the pollution levels of Manhattan. As they moved north, they passed beyond the poisoned winds that blew from the chemical fogs of the New Jersey flats. Harry had deliberately left the Thruway and was on back roads through rolling dairy country.

Ellen sat close to the opened window, letting the wind whip the scarf around her throat and toss her hair about. And Harry settled into the anodyne of driving, becoming part of the machine around him, smiling to himself now and then as the suspension leveled out some particularly bad bump. It was a period of rest for them, and they needed it badly. For the moment, the dark clouds of the future seemed to retreat beyond their mental horizons.

Then a particularly vicious thought from one of the houses along the road tore away the peace. Ellen sat up, her face whitening as the jolt triggered her memories. An image came into her mind of a small, twisted man who had been in the library.

Harry sent a questioning probe, and she opened herself to him.

He cursed himself for having sent her there. Grimes was right. He had no business letting Ellen do his dirty work!

The ugly little man had done nothing; he hadn't even tried to get close to her. But his thoughts had been a chaos of utter evil. Unquestionably, he was one of their kind, long since gone mad. But his paranoia was masked by a cunning that made him useful to the flourishing drug business, and he was protected in his insanity. He was safe in his evil—but his mind gibbered and screamed within itself, sensing every hate from the lesser evils he served and fearing the discovery of other mutants. He would have killed Ellen, except for his greater fear of what his masters might do to him.

Maybe the mutants should be cleansed from the race; maybe it was a bad trail for humanity to take. But Harry forced the thought from himself. He could not be sure of all his facts. Even less was he sure of his interpretations of them, in this thirdhand view. And a false analysis of true facts might be worse than a correct interpretation of errors.

Most of the mutants Harry had found were essentially decent—more so than seemed to be normal for humanity. At least, they were before the stresses of their inner instability drove them mad. And while the psi powers could do great harm, that was true of every development man had ever made, from fire to the chemistry that produced both destructive drugs and saving antibiotics.

Now the dairy country changed, and they were driving into an area of rich estates. There were no longer bare fenced pastures along the road or fields of stubble where corn had been harvested for the multitudes of silos. Here most of the country seemed fairly well wooded, with the trees thinned and kept carefully, running down to the roadway to hide most of the mansions that sat back in peace and privacy. The few cars were all expensive, except for those that were somehow ostentatiously small and cheap. Many of the properties had hedges, some in shaped evergreens that must require teams of men to maintain.

Harry slowed, studying the numbers on the mailboxes. Now they were beside a row of hemlocks that grew close together so that no vision could break through them. The hemlocks parted only for a massive wrought-iron gate. Harry spotted the quiet sign and turned in. The gatekeeper was soft-spoken and polite, but very thorough in checking his papers and calling over the telephone in his gate lodge. Then he smiled even more politely and pressed the button that let them through the gate.

"I've seen the invoices," Ellen confirmed Harry's thoughts. "It costs Uncle Charley more for this than the income he used to send you." She sighed. "Most of it is his own money. I think he must have loved her once."

There had been a hint of that when Grimes had shown his mother's picture to Harry. But it was no concern of his. His thoughts were tightening against what he might find here.

Everything went well enough at first. He was checked again in the reception room that might have been the lobby of some unusually fine Swiss inn. Then he was guided by someone named MacAndrews—obviously a doctor, though they called him a counselor—through soft-carpeted hallways toward the most distant wing of the main building.

There were no uniforms here, except for one military one that must have belonged to a visitor. Harry tried to hold his powers down to make sure that none of the thoughts here impinged on his mind, but enough crept through for him to be aware that the staff-to-patient ratio was very high. Then something dark and slimy seeped into his mind, and he had to fight desperately to hold his outward calm and force the unwelcome images away.

"Better let me go first," MacAndrews suggested softly. Without waiting for a reply, the doctor moved toward the end of the hall.

He was barely at one of the doors when a shriek ripped across Harry's mind and was echoed more faintly in his ears. Something caught at him, sucked him into an endless tunnel, then spewed him forth. Clawing terror cut at his entrails, while his mind seemed frozen in a block of dry ice, ice with a dark fire at its core. He staggered, grabbing at the walls for support.

MacAndrews was back at his side, somehow supporting him. The man was obviously a telepathic blank, but his face was surprisingly understanding.

"I'm afraid . . ." he began. Then he didn't bother finishing.

From somewhere, at a signal Harry hadn't noticed, another man appeared, heading toward the doorway at a quiet trot. MacAndrews began guiding Harry away, toward the reception room.

A woman was in Harry's mind, screaming and begging to hide, but clearly to be seen in a mirror over a quilted table. Her face was slack and fat and filled with horror. And then beside her in the mirror was a grotesque and distorted picture of Phil Lawson, threatening her. He saw himself in a child's suit. Ellen seemed to grow before him, distorted, lascivious, evil. Then the picture blotched and ran, foul corpse-decay spilling into symbols of darkness and death.

*Kill the cub that cawls encumber!*

He was on the stairs of a house, with fire spreading from draperies to furniture and running across the carpet, a smell of smoke and kerosene in his nose. He was screaming and trying to climb higher, away from the smoke and heat. But a younger version of the woman in the mirror was clutching his knees, holding him back, urging him to breathe deeply of the smoke to defy the devil, smiling with a horrible desperation. He was trapped in her arms . . .

"Harry!" Ellen's mental voice cut across the picture, driven into his mind by more power than he'd known she possessed.

He grabbed at her thoughts, pulling stability into himself from her. And abruptly the horror was gone. There were only the steps leading from the reception area toward his car, and Ellen's hand on his arm, guiding him. MacAndrews was moving away, saying some last thing to Ellen that Harry could not catch. Then he was getting into the passenger seat while Ellen started the car, her unfamiliarity with it unimportant as she drew its operation from his mind. The big gate opened for them, and they were back on the road.

She started to stop at the first bend, but he was beginning to control himself at last. "I'm all right, Ellen."

He felt her mind examining him, and then a gradual relaxation as she sensed his returning strength. "Do you want to drive, Harry?"

"No." She was doing as well now as he could, and his hands were still weak from his previous tension. But the shock was past.

"She was lovely once, even though she always hated

117

me," Ellen said, as the image of the woman in the mirror slid through his mind again fleetingly.

He nodded, letting the memories of his childhood creep up slowly from the blocked area where the barrier had finally broken. Most of them were still incomplete. But Martha Bronson had been a lovely woman—as cold and lovely as an ancient statue. And Harry's father had been a handsome man. He was still attractive enough, though the face that the world knew now as Dr. Philip Lawson was far more furrowed than Harry remembered it.

"So that is the end of their roads," Harry said harshly.

For his mother, madness that was a horrid blaze to equal all the icy reserve that had been her sanity. And for her, even madness had not blotted out all of her psi ability but had left shreds of it to point up the decay of her soul and to make her aware of the ugliness of her fate.

And for his father, as he now recognized the man . . .

Philip Bronson had been perhaps the most gifted surgeon of his time, aided by the extrasensory abilities that he had used with the most scrupulous ethics for the aid of those who needed his skills. Now, as Philip Lawson, he was cured of his madness—and of all that had been great within himself.

Harry remembered the doctor's house with its glaring neon sign and the man's pitiful cynicism about his own unethical practice, his need to denigrate himself in order to avoid a rejection of his invitation by the son he no longered dared to admit was his.

Those were the two alternates for most of those with the mutant gifts they had never sought and could not put aside. And for himself and Ellen, after two more months . . .

# XI.

## HATE

Back in the living quarters, Gordon could hear Kim putting the youngest boy to bed, and his face lighted briefly at the familiar sounds. Then he sobered again, to go on with his slow pacing across the floor of the room he had turned into an office. Almost idly, he noticed that his hip was hurting worse tonight. Mostly now, he didn't notice it; after the bullet had shattered the joint, ending his career on the force, the doctors had done a great job rebuilding it. Maybe it was the weather.

He knew better, however. And he knew it wasn't the day spent out in the worst slums of Newark. That had reminded him a little too much of the shack in which he'd been born, before his mother managed to move up North to Harlem, but those weren't all bad memories. A kid can enjoy almost anything, particularly when his friends are no better off. There hadn't been television then to tell them how the other folks lived.

Maybe he should drop this damned case. His suspicions were beginning to make him goofy. But young Bronson was a good man to work for, and he paid promptly and without kicks. It was steady money—steady work for almost a month now—and he'd need that for the lean periods.

Kim came in with fresh glasses for the tiny bar in the office, and he smiled again for her benefit. She was the only good thing that had come out of that mess in Korea to which they'd sent him by a trick, just when he'd finally been promised the law school scholarship. That had ended his first set of dreams. It was too late for more schooling when he'd come back with Kim and a young son—and they'd tried to make a stink about that, until his colonel fixed it for him. So there had been fourteen years with New York's finest, before the bullet from the young punk got him.

He heard the sound of steps outside the door he'd had installed to his office and headed for it before the buzzer sounded. "Keep your nose clean," he told himself. It had always been his motto, and now was no time to forget it. What lay behind Bronson's job was none of his business. Maybe he couldn't help getting some hints, but he didn't have to work at figuring it out.

"Sorry to keep you so late," Bronson apologized as he entered.

"You're paying for it," Gordon told him, grinning quietly in the automatic response. But it came hard this time. "Everything's on my desk, so you might as well sit there. Unless you want to take the papers with you?"

He knew the answer to that, of course. Bronson would want him around while the reports were studied. Sometimes there were side bits that came up only in discussion which seemed important to the client. He watched the man slip behind the desk and forced himself onto the couch at the side of the room, putting himself out of Bronson's direct line of sight—as if that made any difference.

Then he couldn't sit still. "How about a drink?"

Bronson nodded absently, and Gordon moved over to the bar, dragging out freshly cleaned glasses and the ice bucket Kim had filled. *Bourbon or scotch?*

"Scotch and water will be fine," Bronson answered.

The only trouble was that Gordon hadn't asked it aloud. He'd shouted it in his mind, but no sound had passed his lips.

So now he knew. Now all his guesses were confirmed.

He finished making the drink by muscular habit. His own drink was simpler; he left it neat. And he was pleased that his hand steadied enough to put Bronson's glass down before the man without making a noise. His hip was killing him now, but he got back to the couch and sank onto it without letting the groan pass his lips.

Mind readers! A bunch of crazy mind readers! A damned bunch of honky mind readers!

He tried to clip the word out of his thoughts, but it stuck there. Sure, he knew it didn't mean anything. It was just corrupted Swahili, where the word had meant simply *white*.

"You let me hear you say that word one more time, I gonna tan you white as snow." His tired mother's voice echoed in his mind, and there was the stench of garbage from the street, the drip of water down the scrofulous wall where the plumbing above leaked, the tap-tapping of the collector's hard, unworn heels down the ancient hall. Honky!

Now they got them this mind-reading trick. Who got it? Honkies got it, that who. We not good enough for that. Ain't no honky gonna give a thing like that to no nigger.

Gordon drained half his glass, and the sharp bite of the bourbon cut through his self-mockery for a moment. But it couldn't still the thoughts; it could barely kill the ancient street language.

Mutations, of course. He'd read about such things; he could guess from his investigations that it had to be the answer. White mutations. There would be no mind-reading genes from his black ancestry and none from Kim's ancient heredity. Harry Bronson and his white wife could have a dozen kids, and they could all read minds. But little Timmy in his bed and Buzz and Trina—there was no magic for them. They didn't have honky parents to give them the inside track from the day they were born. Let one of them put a bullet through a white man's hip and see how lenient the judge would be!

He grunted in self-disgust and downed the rest of his liquor. Damn it, the punk had been white, but he'd been trying to shoot Gordon's partner, who was also white; it was only the drug-deprived shakes that had sent the bullet into black flesh. And the white men at the draft board who'd fouled up his student deferment hadn't even known he was black.

He'd had too many white friends and too many good experiences with white men to hate them. He'd gotten over all that nonsense before Korea was done. He'd sworn to his mother on her deathbed that he didn't hate anyone, and he'd meant it. He'd lived it, too.

Bronson threw aside a paper in a disgusted manner and glanced up to where Gordon was sitting. He muttered something, too low to be heard.

And Gordon found himself on his feet, starting to nod his head in the old gesture. "Yes, sir, boss," he felt his lips shaping silently. Yes, boss; you right, boss; thank you, boss.

And even up here in the North, when he was already twelve: "I catch you scowl like that again at white folks, I lick you down to bones, you hear me? You better hear me good. 'Cause I don't bring me up no sassy kids, not here nor nowhere! White folks speak to you, you smile and you act polite." Twelve? Other memories came back from the time when he was in the last year of high school, coming home with one of his few white teammates. "Don't you ever 'man' nobody! Ever! Don't make no difference, they call you 'boy.' Don't make no difference you don't mean nothing, all in fun, all that stuff. You don't 'man' him, you hear?"

And now they were in his mind. Couldn't even "man" them there anymore. Sure, looked like they might flip after a while, but meantimes they had him by the balls for certain. And someday, when they got the bugs ironed out of the mutation, they'd have an edge nobody could beat. Equal rights then for sure—equal for all honkies!

He hobbled to the window, fighting the scream that was building up inside him. Out there, the light was out; it was almost black on the street—black and dirty and bare. His street—his one way street to nowhere.

Gordon bent forward, swaying with what was in his guts too deep to let out. And from somewhere, there was an arm

122

around his shoulder and a white hand was gripping him and holding him.

He turned slowly, burying his head against Bronson's white shoulder, beating his black hands against his thighs, sick with hate for the hate that he thought he'd lost half a lifetime before.

## XII.

## ALIEN

The afternoon session of the symposium on chemical psychopathology was starting, and some of the crowd of learned men were beginning to move toward the lecture room or away on business of their own. Harry found no one left whom he'd hoped to meet. He looked at his watch, sighed in the habit he had begun developing, and headed for the bar.

Time, he thought bitterly. It was a constant weight on his thoughts now. The months had dwindled down, leaving only a few days ahead for the impossible task. How many days was uncertain, but the number was too small. For some reason, neither he nor Ellen could pinpoint the exact date of the final break into madness; it was as if the whole subject left a vagueness around itself through which no sharp insight could be had. But the date was horribly close.

He found Dr. Hirsch nursing a sixth katinka and exuding importance together with an odor of apricot brandy. The psychiatrist looked up vaguely as Harry approached. The man who had undertaken the treatment of a shocked and amnesiac boy had proved to be only a bore, not the terror that memory painted him. He had been almost pathetically pleased at being remembered when he received Harry's note. Now he had served his purpose in introducing his former patient to the other psychologists and psychiatrists attending, and he was entitled to a polite leave-taking, even if he was too foggy to appreciate it.

"Ah." Hirsch tapped his second finger five times against the table, then nodded. "Ah, yes. Bronson. Learn anything? Not that you could, with all those—ah, chemists—taking up the whole morning. No sensitivity there, my boy. All technical jargon and formulas. Can't put the human mind into a test tube or paper progress reports, I always say." He switched to his index finger and tapped out another five strokes. "Ah, umm. Did I give you a copy of that article I did on your case?"

Harry reassured him, made his thanks, and got away as quickly as he could. The lecture room was half full as he passed it, though few seemed to be listening to the talk on serotonin precursors. There was a new table covered with brochures from the drug firms, but Bob Gordon had already collected everything pertinent the day before and would be tracing any leads in them through experts.

Ellen joined him in the lobby, her mind nestling comfortably against his as he took her arm. Automatically, they searched each other's thoughts for anything that might have been useful, then gave up together. She had circulated around among the lesser men while he had used his introductions to stay close to the inner group who were considered important by their fellows. But the morning's work had been another waste of time.

It had been a forlorn hope at best, once their first quick scan of the meeting had proved that no mutant was among them. Statistically, there should have been at least one man trained in psychology who was either a mutant or sufficiently empathetic to understand and offer help in the solution of their problem. It was another case of looking for expert assistance, once they recognized their own limitations as amateurs.

In this matter, however, there seemed to be no experts. The men attending the conference were singularly blank to empathy and totally lacking in any extrasensory talents. Apparently their very lack of such abilities to understand their fellow human beings had led them to the futile, formal study of some branch of psychology. And if any of them had treated patients who were mutants, their minds contained no sign that they had recognized any difference from standard psychoses. Certainly there was no hint of any curative techniques beyond palliation that must fail or shock treatments that were too drastic to permit the mutated powers to survive.

All roads seemed to end in blind alleys. Gordon's shock of discovery had been disturbing but had proved to be fortunate in the long run; once the initial hostility had been drained, his deeper understanding of what was wanted had greatly expedited their work together. Yet the results had been only an increase in the number of proven failures. Coleman's list had been expanded, and still there was no evidence of any cured case. Even the reports of the mystics and cultists had been examined, with a few additions to the number of real mutants, but without other progress. Those who had enough talent to be considered mutants either died young—sometimes suspiciously—or ended in the maze of insanity. There seemed to be no exceptions.

In a way, perhaps, that had one good side result. There were none left to become prey to any Alien Entity, so he had gradually accepted the idea that no possession had yet been completed. But that was cold comfort. It might be a sign of incipient paranoia for him to assume that he was either the first or the only one facing such a threat, but it seemed to fit what facts he had. Other mutants had felt some grotesque danger from which their minds must flee, but their fears had come in the form of devils, humans, and fantasies that bore no relation to the alienness he had faced briefly.

A tension in Ellen broke into his guarded thoughts. He had been lightly linked into her mind, letting her guide him along the street while his concealed thoughts moiled over his worries. They had long since found that one mind was enough to cope with such automatic things as moving along streets. Now he became aware that they were mixed into the crowds on Forty-second Street; her unease was somehow related to that. He started to probe gently, but she shook her head and motioned to the approaching bus.

Normally, he would have insisted on a cab. Buses had

always made him somewhat uncomfortable, though he knew that Ellen often took them when he didn't drive her around. He caught a slight insistence in her thoughts, together with some carefully veiled fear. With a shrug, he followed her to an empty seat toward the rear.

By the time the bus turned up Eighth Avenue he was uncomfortably aware of the reason for her insistence. The seats had filled rapidly, and some riders were standing. But the seats behind and before him had remained vacant. When they finally filled, their occupants seemed curiously uncomfortable; the fat man ahead of him turned to stare back at Harry, seemingly puzzled at finding nothing objectionable. At the next stop, he hastily moved to another seat that had been vacated.

Somehow during the long weeks, Harry's mind had developed an ability to shut out almost all of the thoughts around him. Now he lifted the screen slightly, then hastily slipped it back. The brief flash had been enough; there were no specific reasons, but around him were unease and uncertain feelings of hostility beyond the normal human resentment of all strangers. And as the bus began to empty, the nearby seats were again vacant.

"Then I'm not getting psychotic?" Ellen asked. It was obvious that she had noticed the reactions around her for some time and had been afraid that it was a private obsession of her own, a prelude to madness.

He sent a feeling of reassurance toward her, but he was more disturbed than he tried to seem.

One of the standard psychoses was a feeling of being hated or resented by those around one. But suppose the reaction was justified by the facts? By the time a paranoid was detected there was a good chance that his conduct really had made people around him resent him. Was his belief still psychotic? And was there any solid evidence that the belief had come before the fact?

Human animals resented those who did not conform to their ideas of proper humanity, as the construction workers had proved in their attacks on the so-called hippies of this city. It wasn't a matter of ideology, either, or they'd have had dozens of other targets; it was a subtler matter of style and manner. And sometime recently, Ellen and he had apparently developed attitudes that set them apart, perhaps by developing a true bond between themselves that could not be shared by most of humanity. Now they were rejected. Soon, perhaps, they would be targets for open hostility.

Was that one of the pressures on the mutants that made madness inevitable? Harry couldn't be sure. There was a simpler reason, anyhow. His reading had made it plain that there was one circumstance more certain to induce mental breakdown than any other: Given a problem that must be solved and no possible solution, almost all individuals were forced into madness. When the madness was itself the problem without solution . . .

Ellen gasped, and her hand caught his, just as her mind closed down to a nearly impenetrable knot of disgust. But the brief flood of surprise had carried enough intelligence to him for him to rise with her and follow her as she made for the exit door.

A wizened little man was just getting on the bus. Deepset slitted eyes were darting about. They spotted Ellen and came to rest, while a flood of terrorized speculation flashed through the distorted mind.

Harry had already caught Ellen's knowledge that this was the twisted creature whose evil thoughts had bothered her in the library. The man had obviously recognized her, and his mind was broadcasting a message of hate and of suspicion that she was following him. He was starting toward her as the exit door finally began to open.

Harry caught the beginning of a thought and turned quickly to meet the enraged eyes. Once, getting fully into Ellen's mind—even with her consent—had been difficult. Time and practice seemed to have improved his power. Now his mind met the barrier, broke through into the twisted mind, and husked it in one fleeting scan. He felt it try to strike back at him mentally, met the attack, and concentrated his own thoughts into a lightning riposte. Then he was stepping from the bus while the little man stopped and stumbled to a seat in abject fear.

Ellen must have followed the engagement, but the concentration of his mind had let only the rough details come through to her. She walked beside him now, shivering faintly. Then she caught herself and began trying to help drain the ugliness of the memories from his thoughts.

"And you call yourself weak!" she said.

He grimaced, recognizing that there was some pleasure in his reaction to her words, but also realizing how defenseless the weakness of the other man had been. Yet there was more than that—there had been a moment when he had felt . . .

He shook the feeling off, wondering about the twisted man. That, he thought bitterly, was a third alternative—to go mad, but to retain both the mutant powers and enough cunning to operate without being recognized as insane. There had been no fight against growing insanity there, but a welcoming of it. No shock had come with the psychoses, but a lust to use himself to revenge his own failures on the world.

If there were even a hundred like him in all the race, then the mutation was a perversion of humanity that deserved to be stamped out. This one was cunning but essentially petty and stupid. A more cleverly evil telepath could probably find ways to seek full vengeance for his fancied wrongs against all mankind. There must be government agencies where a mental spy could find a welcome, and where his slight twists of facts could trigger a rising holocaust.

A difference of language was an obstacle to reading minds, but not a permanent one. Thoughts could be clearly read only in the language the reader knew, but so much of the basic meaning trickled through that gaining fluency in another tongue was a matter of only a few weeks of slight effort. Harry had already begun to pick up a smattering of Spanish before he learned to control his reception of outside thoughts.

They were almost to the apartment building when there was a squeal of brakes ahead of them. Harry looked up to see a car being hastily parked at the curb. He smiled at

129

sight of the worried face of the driver and headed for the car as Ellen went into the building. His smile broadened as the man caught sight of him.

"I took the bus from the meeting," he called out to the surprised investigator. "We got off at Columbus Circle and walked the rest of the way. Put that in your report. You didn't miss anything."

The man from the agency employed by Grimes hesitated, then grinned back at him. "Thanks, Mr. Bronson. Thought I'd lost you back there. Bob Gordon tip you off I was on your tail today?"

Harry nodded, though he no longer needed to be tipped off; he had traced back to the agency and now routinely checked up on the daily assignments each morning. The ability to read minds at greater and greater distances seemed to have grown as steadily as his power to suppress all the unwanted thoughts that reached him. The promise of power suggested by his childhood ability to converse over long distance with his father was nearing full development. He might have enjoyed his increasing ability, except for the constant awareness that there would never be time enough to realize it fully.

Ellen was busy with a shopping list when he entered the apartment, but she had already started the coffee. He waited until it was down, then dropped to a seat beside her, pondering over the incident on the bus. He had a faint awareness of her mind touching his to learn his desires for dinner, but most of it was below his fully conscious level; by now she could trace his appetite better than he could. He watched with a familiar amusement her decision to go out shopping rather than call in her order. Shopping and cooking were her chief relief from the growing tensions of their marriage.

After she was gone, he faced himself more fully than he'd wanted to do while her mind was so close. He'd been scared by the potential for evil in the twisted man. Now he realized the danger that his own mind might represent, if his thoughts were aberrant. He was sure that his mental powers, already far stronger than those of the other, were still growing rapidly. He had been careful in his use of them so far—but would he always control himself? In a few days, when madness struck, would he lose those powers—or would he pervert them into the savagery that lay too close to all mankind's background?

He knew too little about the mutation. Most of the mutants he had identified who were still sane had seemed essentially far more decent than the average of humanity. He had found little dangerous desire for power. Yet there had been Miss Jamieson and the man on the bus. How many others might there be with potential for harm?

There was little communication between him and Ellen through the dinner. He felt her private internal struggles over some horror of her animal self that had been triggered by the contact with the twisted man; he respected her wish for privacy in her thoughts, just as she let him argue out his own questions alone. But it made for a temporary feeling of isolation between them that was strongly unpleasant. He watched with some relief as she finished the dishes and went to lie down. Then he decided to walk over to Gordon's office. The report on the drugs listed in the brochures should be ready for him.

Harry was heading toward Broadway when he first sensed that something was wrong. He hesitated, sending a questioning probe toward Ellen. She was still sleeping, undisturbed, but the feeling of danger did not abate. He turned back, beginning to run as he neared the apartment building. He passed the entrance and darted down a narrow alley to the rear.

The twisted little man was a motionless shadow, huddled on the fire escape below Ellen's bedroom. Then, as he recognized Harry, he sprang up and dropped the mental screen with which he had been trying to conceal his intentions.

His mind was driven by amphetamines into a concentrated blast of rage and vengeance. These two had spied on Ziggy; they were after him. But he had traced their minds, and now they'd pay. First the woman, once he kicked in the window. Ziggy would have her before the man could reach him.

There was no time for a physical rescue. Harry struck

131

out with his thoughts, forcing himself to meet the filth that poured from the septic mind. But this time Ziggy was not caught unaware. His defenses gave slightly, but he was mentally braced, hopped up by his triumph and the drugs that dulled his fear.

Harry threw all the fury of his desperation into an effort to stop the creature. He saw the foot move, and he concentrated every thought against it, holding it . . .

Then he lay collapsed on the ground, staring upward helplessly, while horror seized him and owned him completely. The Alien Entity of his precognition was inside his head, taking over his mind and shoving him aside. He was cut off from all telepathy, locked away in a corner of his mind, totally helpless!

From the back of the mind that had been his, Harry tried to scream a plea to the presence that had seized him. But the alien horror he had felt briefly was shielded from him now. His possessor had cut itself off from him, as it had cut him off from all contact with other minds. He was aware of only a pressure of ruthless power that was beyond his understanding.

He could no longer control his muscles, but he could still hear and see. His eyes turned without his will and came into focus on Ziggy. And suddenly the veil over Harry's perception was lifted enough for him to read some of the thoughts of the little man, though all other minds remained closed to him.

Ziggy was gloating in anticipation as his leg swung far back for the kick that would smash the window and let him in to find the woman. But the kick was never completed. The foot came down gently beside his other one. With a grace he had never shown before, he turned from the window and began descending the iron steps that led from landing to landing.

The shock of that produced a complete hiatus in Ziggy's thoughts. Then his brain flooded with rage, and he struck out with all his twisted powers.

His effort was wasted. He kept walking gracefully down the steps, and now something was happening in his perverted mind. His telepathic ability began to fade away, as if drained through a hole in his brain. At the end of the first flight, no power remained.

Next his memories began to vanish, beginning with his earliest, moving forward year by year. His childhood was gone, his adolescent years, and the loss moved forward across his warped adult life. He was drooling and cursing now as he moved down the flights of stairs. Yet always, something was left; one part of the mind remained untouched, left to let him know what he was losing.

Mercifully, Harry's awareness of the man's torture had been growing weaker. Only his eyes and ears told him what was happening as Ziggy reached the last landing. The little man dropped from there to the ground with the same strange grace and stood erect, mouthing futile curses. Then his body slumped, and the curses changed to a meaningless, bleating cry. He went stumbling away, his face now slack and empty.

Harry forced the sickness from his mind and drew further into himself, trying to prepare himself for the battle he must wage to regain control. He was shivering from the dampness and cold of the ground, and his shoulder ached from the pressure of some bit of rubble. He tried to sit up—and his body obeyed his wishes.

The Alien Entity was gone; he was again alone in his head!

He moved back into himself, fearing some kind of a trap. His mental landscape felt disturbed, touched with an alienness that was beginning to fade. But there was no sign of any other presence. He felt gently for Ellen's mind. She was sleeping quietly. Somehow, the grisly events had been kept from her.

He wanted desperately to go to her, to seek comfort and to regain his stability. But this was no burden to put upon her. He stood there, fighting it out within himself, until he could control himself to walk back down the alley and away, beyond the reach of her sleeping thoughts.

He found a nearly vacant restaurant on Broadway and went in, taking his coffee to the privacy of the back booth.

There was no pattern he could find. The Alien had taken him without effort when his mind was occupied with Ziggy.

Then, for no reason he could determine, it had simply vanished back into the future from which it had struck.

The future? His thought seized on that, looking for evidence. He could find none, yet he was completely certain that the idea was correct. The thing did not exist in the present. It lay in his future, waiting for him there. And from that future, it could reach back to take him and to use him with a power beyond his own and in ways that left him still quivering with horror inside himself.

Coleman had suggested that precognition was simply telepathy working through time, permitting a man to read his own future thoughts. It should be theoretically possible then for the future mind to reach back to the past. Perhaps some memory worked that way. But reading a mind was not the same as taking total control of it.

For what purpose? Why had the Alien struck—and even more puzzling, why had it simply vanished again? How far in the future did it lie?

Harry could find no answers. Nor could he discover anything more about the nature of the possession. There must be traces left in his mind, but he could not force himself to accept them. His mind was already trying to blank out what memories it had. And maybe putting it all aside was the best thing to do; his faint hope of winning against foreseen insanity could hardly be helped by an endless process of asking questions for which he had no answers.

All he had gained was an uncertain belief that the risk of possession lay beyond the threat of madness. He had to fight against the first before worrying about the second.

He shrugged unhappily and left the restaurant, heading again for Gordon's office.

Kim let him in. "Hello, Harry. Bob's making some coffee. He expected you."

She knew of his abilities, but the knowledge seemed a matter of total unimportance to her. She bustled about, smiling and quiet as always, until she was sure he was comfortable. He could hear Gordon's voice from the main apartment, busy putting the younger boy to bed.

The investigator came in a few minutes later, carrying a tray. He poured for Harry, then took a cup for himself,

134

black and heavy on the sugar. "The one thing Kim can't do is make good coffee," he said automatically. "You look at the summary I wrote up? It's no dice, Harry."

Harry had already glanced over the report on the one drug that had seemed slightly promising, offering a hope of controlling some forms of schizophrenia without too much sedation as a side effect. Gordon's notes on it indicated that it might be effective in controlling Ménière's syndrome—whatever that was—and preventing travel sickness, but that it had failed all further tests. Either the first report had been biased or incompetent, and it was no better than most other tranquilizers in dealing with psychoses.

"How'd you get the current reports on it?" Harry asked. He had accepted so many failures already that one more hardly touched him.

"Their head biochemist is a militant. When I let him know how I'd been shot by a white punk, he adopted me as a soul brother. That report was just in; they haven't had time yet to retract their first release." Gordon hesitated, then sighed softly. "Harry, how much longer do you think you'll need me? I've got . . . Oh, hell, take a look and see for yourself."

It was obvious that Gordon meant to stick to the bitter end if it would help in any way. But he could see little left for him to do. And now the Acme people wanted Gordon on a long-term industrial job. It was a good deal for him. Yet he was almost hoping that Harry might find an excuse to keep him on and to hell with security. There was a feeling that had grown imperceptibly between the two men without any need for discussion.

"Better sign on with Acme," Harry told him. He found Gordon's last statement among the papers on the desk and glanced at the figure. There were a fair number of items missing from it, such as the times after hours here, but he'd expected that. He made out the check for the amount of the bill without comment and watched Gordon toss it into the drawer.

"Kim always knows how to find me," Gordon said. "Any time, Harry."

"I'll keep in touch—if I can," Harry promised.

The investigator nodded soberly, keeping his hand on the door knob. "Do that."

Harry headed across the dark street, feeling the future narrow down ahead of him. A man should feel the present add to his past, but each bit of present now seemed to strip something from him. Even precognition refused to come now, as if there was nothing ahead to induce memories back to him—or nothing his mind would accept.

Then he remembered one earlier bit of precognition that had not yet been fulfilled. It seemed a good time to take care of it; he was in no mood to return to Ellen yet. He grunted and turned back toward an avenue where he could find a cab heading downtown. The event he was now heading toward was one he had once tried to reject. But its horror had diminished in comparison to other things, and he could now find no other alternative. He no longer could be sure that his future self had any better reason for the decision than he had, but since nothing seemed to offer a better answer, he was past letting such things bother him. Anyhow, if precognition worked, he was committed to the action, and it made more sense to be ready for it than to have to depend on hasty expedients later.

The skill of the experts had proved to be only the clumsy art of men stumbling through darkness. The drugs of the accepted pharmacopoeia were useless to him. Perhaps he might be forced to try the experiments of fools and the palliative of hopeless escape.

Dave and Tina Hillery were delighted to see him, once he assured them that he hadn't mistaken this for a meeting night of the Primates. For half an hour, he relaxed and almost recovered his old attitudes. Then Tina's gossip began to bore him, and he discovered that one bottle of Dave's bargain beer was enough. Dave's latest book was doing well, surprisingly, but the man's self-chosen poverty could not be broken by anything as simple as money.

Dave listened in openmouthed surprise as Harry broached the real reason for his visit. Then his face hardened.

"Not a chance. I'm not prissy—you know that, Harry. But

136

the stuff is no damned good. It's a weakling's copout on a world he hasn't got guts enough to enjoy for itself. It's god in a powder; only the god turns up later with horns and tail."

"Okay," Harry said quietly. "I guess I can get it through Galloway. His last couple of articles were on the private drug scene."

"Galloway! He got all that from me, and he got it wrong. He wouldn't know a male leaf from a female, nor pot from hash. You'd pay through the nose for dope you got through him. And you'd wind up with real trouble. Right now, there's more stuff cut with strychnine than you'd believe."

"So I'll have to take my chances." He felt the resistance begin to melt and turned to Tina. "I'm sorry to bother you people, but I always heard Dave could make contacts better than anyone else."

Dave refused to be baited. He had no need to prove himself, since it was generally recognized that he knew more of what had once been the Village than any other man living there. But Tina gradually swung to Harry's side. At last, Dave gave in. He took the money reluctantly, whistling in amazement at the amount Harry wanted.

"You can't use all that, Harry. What's up? You getting this for one of Fred Emmett's crazy parties? I heard his group was turning on since Nora Bley moved in with him. You're not hanging around that pack of dogs, are you?"

Harry shrugged. "Does it matter? But I'm not seeing Nora, if you must know. I'm still satisfied with married life."

"Okay, it's your business, Harry." Dave considered carefully, glancing at a note-jammed calendar on the telephone table. "Hash, seeds, mescaline, LSD—I can get all of it. But the good stuff is a little short right now, I hear. A lot of it is pure poison; a kid last week ruptured his appendix in convulsions and was too blotto to realize it. Even the pure quill is risky enough; some people get bad trips on anything. Umm, well, if you insist—give me through day after tomorrow and I'll probably have everything."

Tina expected Harry to stay for more socializing, but he was saved from further gossip and beer by the arrival of two other Primates, who wanted to start a literary bull session with Dave. He let Dave lend him a book on drugs, full of warnings and facts, but also giving detailed instructions. Then he managed to break away.

Ellen was asleep when he reached the apartment. Her mind was troubled with vague feelings of some ugliness, but it was not concerned with Ziggy or with anything she sensed from Harry. He broadcast a generalized feeling of warmth and affection toward her and felt her respond by drifting into more comfortable sleep. He closed the hall door and began making the inevitable pot of coffee, glancing through Dave's book while he waited. The warnings only confirmed his feelings against the so-called psychedelics, but he put aside his repugnance and carefully memorized the details of their use. Then he slipped the book into an inconspicuous spot among some technical manuals and turned to his coffee.

A thin feeling of a multitude of other minds was a faint wash under his thoughts. Fear, anger, hate—such emotions were bubbles breaking sharply on the dark surface. There was an ugliness to humanity, but greater experience had taught him to sense and admire the potential for development and greatness and to discount the animal that still lay in the racial background. Then a clear, clean thought touched his mind.

It came from a boy who had just begun to realize his mutant powers and had found a girl recently with the same ability. So far there was no precognition of madness; that would almost certainly come later. Now the flame of the boy's mind burned cleanly and with a strange sweetness that seemed almost the perfect development of the human potential Harry cherished.

He leaned forward to pour another coffee, considering the nature of his kind again. His experience was limited to a rather small number, and most of them had been old enough to have grasped the evil of what seemed to be their inevitable destiny. What were the mutants really like initially?

Surprisingly, he found that screening out normal thoughts and opening himself only to the thoughts of other mutants was much easier than he could have expected from the uncertain theories he had formed. If thoughts were radiated on some strange spectrum of frequencies, then the mutants used a different polarization or band, though there was an overlap between that and the normal frequency range. When he groped for their thoughts, they stood out easily from the great background of the rest of humanity. His reach was still limited, but it was great enough now to take in most of the five boroughs of the city.

The number of such minds he could sense was only a tiny fraction of the population, but it was higher than he had expected. There were many with only a trace of the power, as if even the third generation had not fully stabilized the mutation. Most of them were young.

Harry realized the reason for that youthfulness bitterly. Death or the blow of insanity lay just beyond the border of youth, waiting to destroy or burn out the abilities in shocking horror. Even a quick sampling showed him no reason to doubt the pessimism engendered by his months of investigation. There was not even a single mind he could reach that had passed into maturity without the shadow of madness; he could find none that had gone beyond that madness to a cure.

Neither was there even one other that was aware of an Alien Entity. Many had some cloudy horror in the future, but all could be explained easily as a part of their own mad fantasies. Again, Harry was forced to decide that he was at least currently alone in risking his future mind to some kind of demoniac possession.

Once or twice, he sensed a faint response, as if the other mind felt his probing, and he drew himself back quickly. But in most cases, the others seemed to have weaker power than his, and he could keep from transmitting to them.

A thumping headache made him stop finally. His brain felt as if he had been stretching it through some rough knothole. He found aspirin and took it with another cup of coffee, considering what he had learned.

There had been evil out there—but far less than he had feared. A very few of the mutant minds were perverted, mostly from the second generation; there was a texture that identified each generation of evolution among them. One of these had been only a slightly lesser evil than Ziggy, but that mind had already gone far into helplessness. In fact, so far as Harry could tell, there had been no really dangerous menace from any of the mutants until they had begun degenerating into psychoses of various types. Even then, they usually suffered from persecution beliefs and were dangerous only to those immediately and intimately connected with them.

Harry's ethical question was answered, at least generally. The mutation represented no basic danger to humanity from wild powers; rather, it seemed that the natural empathy of the mutants led them forward in the great climb upward from the dark animal background of mankind. The few precocious children who had enough power to be detected had been singularly free from the rest of humanity.

If that could be preserved . . .

Harry sighed, feeling the old pressure of problems that must be solved and for which there were no solutions. The only sure way to produce stability in the mutants would be to bring up the children without the twists of the conflict with normal society. But that would require a first generation of stable adults to lead them, which could only be produced by stable leadership during *their* childhood years!

It was hard enough for normal children to grow into maturity, even now. Yet they had the experience of thousands of gernerations of adults to guide them, and they were surrounded all their lives by those who had already made the change.

He felt Ellen's mind reaching for him. She had partially wakened and groped for him, to find his side of the bed empty. Now she was seeking him.

He sent a reassuring message and rinsed his cup and the pot, then turned toward the bedroom. She had already moved in her sleep, making room for him. He slipped in carefully, turning toward her and placing an arm lightly over her, while he felt her thoughts slide down toward the relaxation of deeper sleep.

To his surprise, his own mind seemed to begin relaxing

almost at once. After all the coffee and strain, he had expected to lie awake for hours. But as he caught her sleep rhythms in his mind, his own patterns quieted and fell into sync with hers.

There was another pattern imposed on his mind when he fought his way up from sleep three hours later. He was gasping for breath, and tears were streaming from his eyes, while his heart leaped frantically. Then he caught control and forced his own mind to take over.

"Harry! Oh, Harry, not yet!" It was Ellen's scared cry from beside him.

He mastered himself and shook his head. "It isn't my madness," he assured her, opening his mind enough to convince her.

It had been a woman mutant's mind that he had not even contacted before. And it had forced itself on him during its first realization that the long-expected madness was falling on it—a moment of rational clarity more dreadful than the aberrations of the past few days. It was the final end of the hope that had persisted, despite all precognition, that somehow it could never happen to her.

Through that despair, he could recognize the same foolish hope in himself. For three months he had known with absolute certainty that dark madness must cut him off from the future, yet always there had been a basic hope that it must not be, could not be—nothing like that could happen to him!

He thrust the thoughts from him and turned to comforting Ellen. She was not deceived by the change in his thoughts, but sensed his desires for her; as usual, she tried to follow his wishes, willing herself to accept the sleep rhythms he was trying to impose on her brain. In a few minutes it worked. She lay sleeping again, though vagrant flashes of thoughts indicated that the trouble was only postponed. He slipped from the bed and dressed quietly, to return to the kitchen table. He didn't want coffee this time, but habit sent him through the motions of making it. He sat, toying with the cup and considering this new development.

He had brought it on himself this time, he realized. In

141

forcing himself to seek other mutant minds from the general flood of thoughts, he had extended his talents one more step—as the ache in his brain should have warned him, since similar headaches had accompanied the other advances. He could still keep out all but the faintest awareness of normal minds, even without conscious control, but the stronger flood of mutant thoughts was now separated and would continue to plague him until his mind learned slowly to blank it down with the other thoughts. He was aswim again in a constantly intruding sea of outside thoughts and impressions.

Even as he sat considering the new situation, the thoughts poured into his awareness. There was an orphan girl in the Bronx wondering how she could explain the slip that had revealed her knowledge of her foster-father's embezzling. A young father in Brooklyn was trying to find some way of explaining to his son why other children in the school must never know of what he could do. A couple across the river in New Jersey were almost calmly planning how they would choose death before their madness rendered them helpless. A surgeon in one of the great hospitals was sitting up through the night seeking some means to convince his fellows that the symptoms he had read in a patient's mind were real.

And in Delaware, Bud Coleman suddenly screamed!

Harry cut that off before the whole picture came to him. The distance should have made reception of it impossible, but some random matching had brought the flash into his mind too strongly for any error in recognition. Mercifully, there was no repetition, nor any other evidence of long-distance telepathy. He could not have taken more than a brief moment of such frantic, unalloyed rapture.

Harry considered and rejected the use of the mind-dulling effects of alcohol. There was too little time left for him to waste any of it in besotted maundering; better the fight to preserve his own thoughts through the turmoil of other impressions than to deaden himself again. At least he had one advantage; at this time, most people were sleeping. He had less to contend with during the first and most difficult hours of learning to handle it.

142

He was sweating it out slowly, drawing on what little he knew of how he had developed a screen against normal thoughts. He began suppressing all outside influences, even the awareness of Ellen. And little by little, he seemed to gain some control. By the time dawn was lighting the kitchen window faintly he felt he had achieved progress.

Then he permitted himself to relax and let the cramped muscles that had accompanied his mental struggle flex and loosen.

The thoughts came flooding back, now in greater number as those who had been sleeping began to waken and resume their daytime worries. He could almost blank them out by effort—but it took most of his ability to do so, leaving him little energy to think about anything else.

He heated the coffee he had been unconsciously wanting for the last hour, and the familiar sound of Ellen getting up and going to the bathroom registered on his mind. The old patterns of daily life were oddly comforting. For a moment, things seemed almost normal. The unwelcome external thoughts were still registering, but they were now buried under the familiar patterns of his own thinking.

Then abruptly, just as he was sitting down to his coffee, there was another presence in his mind.

This was no demoniac possession. There was no horror of an Alien Entity, no fear. It was a calling to him that he knew he could reject. But he felt no need to thrust it away.

There was a great wave of something utterly strange that drew his whole psyche to it and dismissed all other intrusions as if they had been erased from existence. Harry felt a sense of incredible distances and tremendous chasms that separated the background of the presence from anything he had ever known. It seemed to be faint and unsteady, yet with an aura of immense certainty and power behind it.

There were no words, no pictures. Whatever it was must be so utterly nonhuman that no direct concepts could bridge the differences between them. Yet there was a sense of supporting warmth behind it and a friendliness that no lack of conceptual symbol could conceal. There was loneliness, too—a vast, compelling surge of desire for con-

143

tact that seemed to cry out across the gulfs between.

It lingered in his mind for a few seconds and then began to sigh away, carrying with it a disappointment free of all resentment and leaving an implied promise to return again—to try and keep trying—but after the passage of some time that Harry could only translate from his emotional response into long years.

Ellen was standing in the door, staring at him, and he turned to her quickly. "Did you hear it?"

"No." She shook her head, gazing at him in perplexity. "I caught something in your mind, but it was . . ." She stopped, and he felt her total lack of understanding.

The flood of external thoughts had returned, demanding his conscious control to suppress them. Now he let himself receive them, searching for any other awareness of the signal. There was none. No other mind seemed to have been touched. Yet he was absolutely sure that the presence had been no aberration of his own mind. Even in total insanity, he could have conceived of nothing like it.

"What was it, Harry?" Ellen asked.

He shook his head, desperately trying to recall the feeling of the presence that was fading from his mind so quickly.

"Total sanity!" he told her. "Somewhere, somehow, some race has gained all our powers and has learned to stay sane—incredibly sane and healthy. My God, how long they must have been sane and in full control! Ellen, it can be done!"

Then the doubts returned to him. Somewhere, it had been done—once! Somewhere in the universe, there were not only Alien Entities who preyed on minds but also beings who had not failed. But the impression of loneliness had carried a bitter knowledge with it, implying that the achievement was unique. How many races around how many stars had found their way to extrasensory powers, only to be taken over or to fail as the pressures of their social heritage drove those with talents into madness? How many geniuses must have fought for the answer—and failed?

He tried to brush his mind free and think again, to use

144

the new knowledge that success was possible as a stepping-stone to the answer. But now the other mutant minds were busy throughout the city, brushing their thoughts against his, wearing away his ability to concentrate on any line of reasoning except the deliberate control needed to keep them out—a control that took so much effort that he had too little reserve for clear thinking.

The thought that had been building for hours came then, unexpectedly, though logically following his earlier acceptance. It was a hopeless chance, but . . .

Ellen gasped, dropping the glass of orange juice as she read his mind. "No, Harry! No, not that way!"

His own fears echoed her misery. But there was no other hope now.

# XIII.

## POWER

The twenty-four-hour timer indicated that it was two o'clock in the morning as it turned on a heater under a small pot of water. A short time later the water began to boil and a buzzer sounded. Charles Grimes groaned and fumbled for the switch, then began forcing himself up. He soaked a tea bag in the water, waited a moment, and sipped the hot brew. As it took effect, he reached for his glasses and started dressing.

There had been a time when he hadn't needed the tea and when he had been instantly eager to begin his nightly trip. Now it was only a ritual through which he dragged his protesting body. Still, habits carried him to the waiting elevator, and his fingers shook only slightly as he turned a key in the slot below the row of buttons.

The private elevator dropped smoothly, the lights indicating the floors they passed. The last light went out, and the elevator sank one more level, where no other could come. The door opened, and Grimes trudged down a short hallway. He fumbled with another elaborate lock, stepped through, and sealed the heavy door behind him.

Fifteen years had passed since he first bought this building. The contractors who had dug this small subbasement room for him must have long since forgotten all the details. No one else had ever known, unless some damned freak had read his mind, despite his efforts never to think of this when one was around.

Fifteen years! He had never missed a night here, whether sick or well. He knew it was folly beyond belief, yet he had persisted and would continue to persist, probably until they buried him. He had nothing else. Not that he deserved better. Any man who gave his heart to a bunch of freaks and their kids deserved what he got.

He sank into a comfortable chair in one corner of the raw concrete walls of the room, resting his eyes on the only other visible feature. The floor was a massive slab of cement. In the center of it, resting on multiple layers of rubber and felt, was a low pedestal. A platform from an expensive record player topped that, beautifully sprung to absorb vibration. And on that sat a bell jar of glass, as highly evacuated as the best vacuum pumps could accomplish. It should be a good vacuum, he thought; getting the equipment in here had cost him enough once.

Inside the jar, a short rod of grounded copper stuck up, with a marble-sized ball of styrofoam resting at the top in a shallow depression. It was the lightest object possible. It rested there so securely that no vibration had ever reached it to jar it from its position. Yet it could be toppled by the force of a grain of dust striking it, if any dust could have reached it.

No other equipment showed, and the room seemed otherwise bare. The beam of light that the ball cut off from an opposite electric eye came from a hole too small to notice, and the cameras and recording devices that monitored it were only small windows in the walls.

Grimes got up, groaning faintly as a twinge of sciatica hit him. By ritual, he went to the concealed doors and began checking the monitor tapes and recorders. Nothing showed there, though his routine tests showed that the machinery was functioning perfectly. That was as it should be.

Once he had thought that the ball wavered. He had gone up to his suite then in an ecstasy of achievement. But the next night, when a measure of sense returned, he had checked his monitors to find only unwavering straight lines from their pens. He had accepted the evidence, to realize

147

that it was only his own mind that had wavered under his inner pressure. Since then, he had permitted no such wish-fallacies to disturb his mental efforts.

He sat down in the old chair again, resting his body against its cushions, letting his head relax back comfortably, and centering his eyes on the small white ball. He no longer needed a clock to check his hour of ritual.

He had gone through every phase of effort. He had tried total concentration, mind-controlling phrases from the mystics, and blank relaxation. Now he merely triggered the thought of his desire in his mind and let his head fill with whatever else might come into it.

They had assured him that he was a complete null in telepathy, and he had accepted the fact. Palermo and Bronson were too eager for more freaks at that time to lie to him. He'd let them stick to their magic while he exercised his own talent in investments and handling money, as well as protected them from all legal troubles. In his own way, damn it, he'd been as good as they were—so good they could never have gotten by without him.

Yet they hadn't fooled him. Under their outward friendship, they'd never considered him their equal. They'd sneered at him, even when they were murdering themselves, going nuts, and handing their poor kids over to him after their failures. They had power, and he had none. Much good it had done them!

Phil Bronson had been the worst, acting as if his medical ethics made him superior to a man whose legal code then was as rigid as the ethics of any doctor. He'd seemed changed since they let him out, of course; he couldn't pull ethics anymore, not with his practice. But Grimes had no desire to be fooled again; he'd told Bronson-now-Lawson off when the man came to take back his guardianship. And he'd made it stick.

Only Palermo had been different. Grimes grimaced bitterly. The thought of the end of that friendship was still too painful for him to dwell on.

And the kids—damn it, he'd tried. No man could have done more, or gotten less thanks for it. The taint had been too deep. Maybe Martha had been right. She'd called it a taint, and she should have known.

He shifted on the chair without moving his eyes from the ball. His sigh echoed hollowly in the room. All right, damn it, he'd still make a fool of himself, probably, if they'd let him. If the kids had enough sense to come to him honestly—but they never would. They had power, too. Much good it would do them, either!

He started to get up, disgusted with his thoughts this evening. Then he shrugged faintly, aware that the hour was not quite up. He dropped back, raising his glance to the ball.

Hesitantly, the little sphere trembled, seemed to shake, and rolled off the rod to bounce on the bottom of the jar!

Grimes felt the sweat spring out on his face. His arms clamped onto the chair as if held by steel bands, and his leg muscles ached as he tensed them. There seemed to be a great hollow in the center of his head that grew and swelled, absorbing all his thoughts. It burst, leaving a greater void behind.

The little ball had come to rest. Now suddenly it stirred again. It lifted half an inch. It lifted again. This time it moved smoothly upward. It hovered over the rod, then settled precisely into place.

Grimes let out his breath explosively. His heart was racing, and his head felt as if it were on fire. His shaking hand on his temple was either too cold or he was running a slight fever. He tore his eyes away, then looked back. The ball still rested on the rod.

Damned fool! Of course; it had never moved, it was simply where it had always been. He had imagined the whole thing!

The traces on the monitors denied that. There were wavers and peaks in the inked lines now. And when he turned on the video tape playback, the screen showed the ball falling, bouncing, and finally reversing itself to settle to rest exactly as he'd seen it happen.

He sighed very softly this time, before beginning a slow circuit of the room. He destroyed the ruled tapes and erased the recording on the video machine. One by one, he turned off the lights and the monitors, until the room was dead and dark. He found the door and went out, leaving it unlocked behind him, to take the elevator back to his suite.

There was still half a cup of tea. He drank the cold liquid gratefully, before turning to the telephone. There was a long wait after he dialed, but he finally heard a sleepy voice answering his call.

"Hello, Phil," he said quietly. "Charley Grimes here. I think we'd better get together as soon as you can get here. It looks as if the kids are getting into some kind of trouble."

# XIV.

## ESCAPE

Dave Hillery was bubbling with good humor this time, though he had probably not been aroused so early in years. Dawn was his usual bedtime. He handed the packet of drugs to Harry without comment. Any disapproval he felt was buried under his enthusiasm for the real-life game of cops and robbers he seemed to think they were playing. It brought out the adolescent romanticism that probably was responsible for the increasing sales of his badly written books. Harry had told him that no real police were involved, but he preferred not to believe it.

He almost tiptoed as he led them down the stairs of the old building. The door into the cellar squeaked and howled in protest, and he glanced stealthily around. They went down rickety steps and across piles of garbage to what was left of an outside entrance. There was a narrow alley that Harry had never seen. A battered old Peugeot was standing there, with barely enough room for the doors to open against the tenement walls on either side.

Dave went to the end of the alley and came back, nodding. "All clear, kids. Good luck, Harry!" He shook his head as Harry started to thank him. "No time, boy! Get going!"

He darted back into the cellar, still almost on tiptoe, as Ellen got into the driver's seat of the old car Dave had managed to purchase from some friend. She smiled faintly, her depression lifting for the moment. She knew as well as Harry that the one man who had tailed them here was still sitting in his car and keeping only a casual eye on the parked Citroën. He'd followed them so long and with so little reason that he probably hadn't even noticed the large suitcase Harry had been carrying.

There was little traffic through the Lincoln Tunnel at that hour, except for a few trucks, and no sign that anyone was following them. The car was no longer handsome, but the engine purred happily. Ellen drove steadily, raising the speed to seventy as they reached the turnpike. But her brief amusement had quickly faded. She was doing what Harry had decided must be done, but her disapproval was a sick weight inside her. Yet she had been forced to agree that there was no other path still open. The doom of madness was a threat that might strike at any hour now.

By the time they shifted to the Garden State Parkway some of the pressure from exterior mutant thoughts began to lift from Harry's mind. Distance was no certain protection, but most of the intruding signals faded back into a vague undercurrent that didn't bother him after a few more miles. He had Ellen stop while they switched places. It was a relief to feel secure enough to drive again without the danger of some violent emotion obtruding at the wrong moment.

Probably they could have moved openly out to Sid Greenwald's deserted house. But Harry was tired of being followed, and he wanted no more petty annoyances interrupting what had to be done. He hadn't even informed Sid of the move, though that hardly mattered; Sid was doing well in his marriage and his new job under König, and the work on the prototype car left him no time to return to America. Dave had insisted on not knowing their destination, of course, so no one should be able to trace them.

They stopped at a supermarket to stock up on the provisions that Ellen had listed, then drove on to the house. It lay back down a short dirt road in sad repair, completely surrounded by trees. At the rear was an old Army munitions dump, and the nearest neighbor was cut off by a tangle of trees and underbrush. Sid had never been close to any neighbors socially, and there was a good chance that no one would ever notice that the house was again occupied.

Ellen gasped when she followed him in. Harry had grown used to it, but his view through her eyes made him realize what a mess it was. Sid had been a sloppy housekeeper at best, and the place had been abandoned to dirt, cobwebs, and dankness for months.

He was grateful that he'd kept the utility bills paid now. He started the basement dehumidifier and turned on the furnace long enough to take the chill out of the house. When he came back up, she was dressed in rough clothes, already puttering with cleaning equipment. He muttered some vague apology she disregarded. But they both realized that the condition of the house might be a good thing. The work would distract her and keep her attention somewhat away from what she feared. Anything that would prevent her maintaining too close contact with him was something of a blessing.

He let his guard relax completely, testing for the presence of any mutant minds nearby. Apparently, he was in better luck than he had dared hope. The only traces he found were from families far enough away to offer little disturbance. By now he was gaining a small measure of automatic control; he might have been able to handle a few intruding thoughts. But the absence of such pressure was the first favorable omen he had found.

He began clearing out the tiny back room in which he had often slept when visiting Sid. There was a decent rug on the floor. He went about tacking padding over the sharp corners of the windowsills, and he unscrewed the doorknob, removing both its danger and the possibility of opening the door from inside the room. Finally he dragged an overstuffed chair from the living room and placed it on the center of the rug. Satisfied with the safety precautions, he began opening the packet of drugs that Dave had obtained for him. Everything was clearly labeled in Dave's scrawl, to his relief.

"No!" Ellen's face was pale under a smudge of dirt as

she stared at him from the doorway. She started toward him, then caught herself. Her desire to accept his guidance fought briefly with her urge to protect him. Protection won, masked by a small cunning that was totally unlike her. "Lunch will be ready in just a few minutes, Harry. Wait until you've eaten."

"No," he told her flatly. His own mind was fighting with itself, and he had no time to argue. They'd discussed the fact that the drugs might work better on an empty stomach, and she knew the time limits as well as he did.

He'd given in to her once already, wasting a day in attempting the only alternative she could suggest. He'd tried sharing minds with her more completely than ever before, forcing his mind down into the horror of the madness she had foreseen for herself. If he could have removed the pressure of the fear of madness that was so much the cause of the insanity itself, she could then have worked on him.

The effort had failed miserably. Their fear had come together, each mind causing a positive feedback reaction that only fanned the flame of fear until it was unbearable. Then she had barely touched his full memory of the Alien Entity and had exploded apart from him in horror. It had been hours before they could link thoughts at all again.

The only good that seemed to have come of it was a tiny shred of possible knowledge. From small indications of difference in their precognition patterns, he felt sure that her attack was to come some indeterminate time before his own sense of horror. That factor, together with her persistent belief that his power was greater than hers, had persuaded her that he must be the one who would take the risk of his plan.

Her eyes pleaded with him a moment more, while her mind threshed about and then surrendered hopelessly. Her shoulders slumped, but her face took on sudden new strength. She threw the mop aside and darted back to find a light chair she could set on the floor facing his.

"Then you won't lock me out," she told him. "I'll sit here."

"Seeing it all may be a lot harder than going through it, Ellen. Suppose you can't take it?"

154

Her face was a mask of resolution. "I'll take it!"

He accepted her presence and tried not to think about it. There were a great many other things he chose not to consider, and her decision was only one more slight difficulty. He began his preparations, reviewing all the decisions he had made.

This was at best like a man in a dark cellar trying to shoot a black cat that probably wasn't there, while armed with an unsafe pistol loaded with buckshot—and without knowledge of which end of the gun to point away from himself.

He had only the ghost of a theory based on no real evidence—or perhaps it was only a hope that there still was hope. He had started with a wish-dream that there was some way of immunizing the mind against insanity. The body could be made immune to many diseases by small doses of some milder form of the same disease. Why not the mind?

There was nothing in any of the literature from the honest psychiatrists he could respect to support his wild ideas. But he had been unable to put them aside. Drugs could create temporary psychoses at least somewhat related to the real thing, and—usually—the user recovered fairly quickly from the effects. In fact, some cases of schizophrenia seemed to be related to the presence of certain chemical substances in the brain.

The bad trip he had caught in another mind once had not been the same as the horror he had felt through precognition. But there were enough similarities to encourage his speculation. If he could induce small attacks of the horror from which he could recover, he would at least be acting on his brain in a manner somewhat like a doctor's treatment against rabies by a series of small injections of weakened virus.

Ellen had been interested in it as a purely theoretical discussion. She had even suggested a possibility of her own. They knew nothing of the origin or the duration of the foreseen madness for certain. It was at least possible that the horror was itself only a particularly bad trip, and that the drug spasms of the mind were all that was needed to fulfill the precognition. Whether such a temporary seizure would be severe enough to ruin the extrasensory abilities was uncertain, but it seemed less dangerous than the effects of the real madness they feared.

She had retreated from her idea when she saw in his mind that he was determined to try it. But her suggestion gave an added reason for the experiment, and he refused to abandon his plan.

It was no solution to the problem of Alien possession. But he had abandoned that problem until the risk of the madness was past. His first duty was to Ellen. If he could protect himself until he could save her, he was willing to accept whatever further danger might lie in wait for him.

He caught himself stalling while his thoughts reviewed familiar ground. For a second, he suspected that she was using her mind to guide him into the delay, but there was no sign in her thoughts. She was closed down about herself in desperate determination, simply accepting whatever he did. And her resolution made him ashamed of his delay.

His concoction was as ridiculous a blend of ignorance and fool ideas as his basic plan. He had devised a mixture of drugs that should, he hoped, give him a wild trip with major hallucinations. Now that it was mixed, the only check on his ideas was to take it.

There were three capsules. He swallowed them rapidly, holding his breath until they were down. He'd intended to smoke the hasheesh afterward, but he had overlooked a pipe; for want of a better idea, he'd simply included some of it with the other drugs. He had no idea of whether it would work that way—or whether it would work too well. But it was down, and he could no longer hold back.

The battery-powered clock in the living room was audible now in the silence of the house. It came faintly to his ears. Otherwise, nothing happened. He sat in the chair, forcing himself to relax as completely as he could. The ticking seemed to grow louder, but he realized that was only a trick of his attention to it. He squirmed about, wishing that he had brought the clock in here where he could see it. More time passed, and it seemed to him that he should have been getting some results; but there was no change he could detect.

There was only the ticking of the clock, a faint sound of wind outside, and once a soft sigh from Ellen, who seemed not to have moved a muscle. He listened to the rhythm of the clock, wondering vaguely why Sid had purchased one that kept three-four time. It didn't keep that very well, either. It was speeding up. That was normally impossible, of course; it must be his own tension, affecting the clock and making it run faster. He hadn't known he had the power before. Telekinesis—the control of objects at a distance. Interesting.

His feet felt far away, and he glanced down at them. They seemed to be no farther than ever, though they had a brighter shine than they should have had. But everything was like that. The colors were brilliant, more vivid than he had ever seen them. Must be the clear country air, letting in the full light of the sun.

The part of his mind not staring at his shoes considered that, together with the knowledge that extreme vividness of colors was a standard reaction of hallucinogens. The drugs were working all right, and he was tripping! It was a good feeling, and the knowledge that it was all a drug trip didn't matter; the colors remained wonderful.

Now he detected action from his right shoe. The laces had begun to move, keeping time to the loud bolero of the clock. One lace was a minute hand, the other end was the second hand, jittering around and around in a circle. The tongue of the shoe darted between them, curling up at the end and trying to stop them.

He didn't like the action of the tongue. He tried to kick the shoe off. After a moment, he discovered he must unlace it first. He hesitated, hating to interrupt the laces. But they had stopped moving. He pulled on one. This time the shoe came off, doing a slow barrel roll in the air. It landed a few feet away and began to crawl toward him. It crawled and crawled, but the carpet was rolling back, letting it get no nearer. He could feel his chair pitching as the carpet rolled under it.

He began to cry then, sorry for the shoe that could not get back. He put out a hand, and his arm stretched and stretched. And then he was somehow on the floor, holding the shoe. There was so much of it, and all of it was shoe. He had never really seen a shoe before, and he stared at it, entranced. It was the essence of all Shoe-ness. He turned it slowly in his hands, admiring the brilliance of the soul of the shoe. His perception went into the shoe and through it, until he could feel the shoe throughout his entire being. And slowly a marvelous awareness came to him. It was *his* shoe, and he could wear it! He started to put it on.

Then the light came. It was whiteness, it was brilliance, it was softness and sharpness. Everything was alive in marvelous white light. The light was everywhere, within the walls and through the walls and beyond the walls. It was infinite, and he could see every marvelous part of it. His vision stretched and stretched, and everything was light around him.

Through the light, the presence came. It was a voice without sound, a voice that was light itself. It came to him, was all around him. He could hear the light now, calling him, and he bowed within himself and waited.

The answer to the problem—some problem that must have bothered him—was so simple, so clean. It was an answer to every problem. He could see the paths of the atoms within the light, and the voice of the light was explaining everything, telling him the problems of the atoms and the solutions. And it was wonderful to know that the same marvelous formula fitted all his own problems.

He sank into the light, let himself be a part of it, a great awareness filling him as he filled it. He bent and twisted, casting out the dross of his being, convulsed with the need to be free. Then he was light, adrift . . . adrift . . .

"Harry!" The sound was harsh and insistent. He raised unwilling hands to cover his ears, but the call came through. "Harry! Please, Harry!"

His heavy body pressed against something, and dull, unpleasant light fell onto his eyes. He started to protest, then sat up abruptly as he made out the hazy shape of Ellen's face near him.

"Paper!" he gasped, the urgency so strong that it cut through his mental fog and forced his lips to shape the words. "Paper and pencil! Quick!"

She frowned and moved away while he concentrated on holding the answer until he could write it down safely. It had seemed so sure, so simple. But now it was beginning to fade beyond his recall, the details going away from him as he tried to shape them into words. By the time she returned, only the feeling remained. He stared at the pen and the note pad blankly, fighting to retain even the ghost of certainty. But nothing would come of the answer. It was like a dream he had once had in which he was speaking brilliant Latin—to awake to his quiz on Caesar with no new knowledge of the language.

Then, the real world impinged on him, suddenly ugly in its twisted solidity. He was on a bed in the master bedroom, and Ellen was beside him, her face taut with worry. The sun was shining with lackluster rays through the blinds, indicating that it was already late afternoon.

"I'm all right," he assured her, though he was unsure of how true the statement was. He raised a hand to rest on her thigh, forcing his reluctant muscles to squeeze reassuringly. She was holding a cup of coffee for him, trying to help him drink it. But now he was able to sit up and take it from her hand. It seemed curiously tasteless, but he finished it.

"Was it—horrible?"

He shook his head carefully, unwilling to meet her mind directly yet. "No. No, damn it, it seemed wonderful. And I convinced myself that I had the answer. How'd I get here, Ellen? What happened?"

The first part of her answer was close to his own memory. But then the time element diverged, and details became different.

"You started making cooing sounds, Harry. You got down like a baby and crawled on your hands and knees to the shoe. When you finally picked it up, you just sat and held it, looking at it for what seemed like half an hour. Your mind was so—so infantile—that I couldn't follow it most of the time. And then somehow you pushed me away from you; it was as if a blanket of snow covered your

159

thoughts and I couldn't get through to you at all. It was awful! You had a look on your face as if you were shining inside yourself. You sat there the longest time, frozen like a statue. Then you started to shake and were sick all over yourself. I think you passed out. I didn't know what to do, except to clean you up and drag you in here. After I got you onto the bed, you seemed to be sleeping, so I decided to let you rest."

From her mind, he caught some impression of her struggles to move him and change his clothes. He couldn't remember being sick; but his shirt was fresh, and the sour taste in his mouth confirmed her story. He sat up, forcing himself to move his lethargic feet to the floor, intending to take her in his arms and comfort her. But it was too much effort.

"You did wake me, though," he pointed out. He stood up, expecting something like the sick dizziness of a bad hangover, but there was no such reaction. His limbs were steady enough despite the feeling that they were moving through thick gelatin.

She nodded unhappily. "You lay there for hours and hours, until I began to get scared. Anyhow, Harry, I've got dinner all ready."

The last thing he wanted was food. But he nodded as he headed for the bathroom. His head felt thick, and his coordination seemed to be off; the light was dull to his eyes, tinged with an unpleasant yellow. Good thing he'd taken on Sid's electric bill and paid the water charges, he thought dully as he ran cold water into the tub. The chill of immersion was less of a shock to his body than usual, but the result was enough to make him feel slightly more human.

Dinner was on the table when he reached the alcove off the kitchen, and the room now looked clean and more homelike than he had ever seen it. He made a conscious effort to smile approvingly at Ellen, determined to act in a reasonably normal way. But the food was only a nuisance to be disposed of as quickly as possible, though he had no feeling of queasiness or nausea.

He had known in theory that the drugs produced few physical aftereffects, but he had failed to accept the fact.

160

There was a feeling of psychological hangover that made him keep expecting the outward signs of illness.

He seemed to be disconnected from his body, and his mind was numbed. Yet the overhanging sense of imminent disaster was not reduced; it lay like a dark cloud over all his consciousness, intruding into every effort of thought. The knowledge that the solution he had imagined was no more than a drug fantasy of sensation without sense had destroyed his ability to hold the threat away from himself. Now all his attempts at hope seemed futile.

"There's ice cream for desert," Ellen suggested. "Or pie—but it isn't very good, I'm afraid."

He shook his head, but accepted the coffee she poured him. Then he glanced up as she turned on the kitchen light and went to draw the blinds over the window. Apparently, his time sense was still somewhat distorted; before the blind was fully drawn, he saw that the shadows under the trees were already bluish with evening dusk. Ellen stared out for a moment, then covered the window hastily.

She had been quiet throughout the meal, and he'd assumed it was due to her acceptance of his mood. But now he studied her for the first time since his awakening, aware that the silence was more than a response to him. Her lips were compressed, her face set into a mask stripped of all expression.

He touched her mind tentatively. There was a veil over her thoughts, made up mostly of minor things, such as the dark stain on the sink, the need to scrub the floor, and the food that had been left to spoil in the freezer. He slipped through those surface thoughts briefly, then drew back. Even the quick contact had shown him that she was gathered into a tight knot, deliberately screening him out from her real self.

He could have penetrated to the core of her mind, but habits of mutual respect kept him from doing so. She sensed his withdrawal and smiled faintly at him, but made no effort to open herself to his deeper inspection.

"Are you all right?" he asked, aware that the question was hardly appropriate. She'd been through too much in watching his aberrant behavior to be anything approaching

161

her normal self. She had sworn she could take it and had done so—but at a price to herself that he could only partially realize.

She nodded, meeting his eyes briefly. "I guess so. Why don't you lie down and rest while I do the dishes?"

"I've wasted too much time," he told her. "I'd better get ready to try again."

She frowned at his answer, started to protest, and then shrugged tautly. "I wish you'd wait until tomorrow," she said simply.

There was so little hope of winning him over in her voice that he hesitated, almost ready to agree with her wish. But the feeling somewhere in his mind that the time was short—too short, much too short—was now too strong to be denied. He reached out to catch her hand in his in a mute apology. She did not return the pressure, and he got up, feeling a guilt that was almost evenly divided between his awareness of the further strain he must impose on her and the time he had wasted. As he left, he heard her begin to clear the table and run water into the sink. The normality of such actions was a relief to him.

The battery clock in the living room caught his attention, and he lifted it from its hook on the wall. He carried it with him into the smaller bedroom and placed it where he could see it easily from the chair where he would sit.

Its ticking suddenly sounded louder, beating out a steady message: "Sick . . . quick . . . sick . . . quick . . . sick . . ."

He tried forcing it from his conscious attention, then found a pillow to place under it to muffle the noise.

He closed the blinds and switched on the overhead light, grimacing as he saw the damp spot on the rug where he must have been sick. The room was ugly in its emptiness, and the padding on the window ledges now appeared ridiculous. His previous preparations had all been a waste of effort, as he should have realized from his reading. The drug trips might have some similarity to certain forms of madness, but they seldom produced acts of violence or deliberate self-damage. His precautions had been caused either by emotional prejudice or an unconscious desire to delay the experience.

Now the fear he had felt was gone. There had been nothing horrible about the aberrations induced by the drugs. He felt no reluctance to return to the feelings he had known.

He swore to himself at the anticipation in his mind. Damn it, there *should* have been horror in that trip. The whole object of his experience had been to force the ugliness of simulated madness on himself, not to experience gratifying delusions. The less he had to fear from the experience, the more completely it had failed. In the long run, the average user might find the greatest danger from the Siren seduction of illusory powers that blurred reality and ruined the judgment needed to cope with life. But there was nothing long-range about his problems. To him, the real risk lay in delay when the only good trip was a bad one!

Something jolted against his mind, too fleeting for more than a lightning impression. Horror, fear . . . But the impression had been human, with nothing alien about it.

His stomach knotted, while his mind raced within itself, seeking the madness that might already be beginning. Then he relaxed slightly, realizing that the source had been external. It had been madness, but not within his mind.

He sent a probe toward Ellen in another lurch of fear. But her thoughts were as he'd last found them—knotted into some inner concentration that was unwilling to accept his intrusion. He felt the swish of hot water over a dish in her hand, however, and let himself relax again. She was finishing the dishes, following a routine that was familiar and right for her.

Then he nodded to himself, remembering that Sid's house lay only a few miles from a state mental institution. The impression must have been from one of the patients there—perhaps even a mutant, since the jolt had been so sudden and so strong.

He let his awareness bury the impression by sliding down a side trail of thought. Once he'd believed that all madness must be like that which he had felt by precognition. But reading and the mental impact of aberrant minds had taught him that the truth was far different.

163

Only the mutants seemed to break suddenly into insanity. That was the wrong word, a legal term only, but there seemed to be no better term. Call it insanity, then. Among the normal, nonmutant human beings, madness usually came gradually. There was no moment of shock to them; long before they could be recognized as insane by society, their thoughts had moved far away from at least some aspects of reality. Their frustrations and fears distorted their thinking slowly at first, and their psychoses often took years to mature enough to affect their outward behavior. There were some recognized patterns to it. Even schizophrenia, which often was a reaction of younger people to the stress of making the adjustment from adolescent to adult thinking, had recognizable advance symptoms.

Bud Coleman had discovered that the mutants differed in the suddenness of the onset of their madness and had tried to devise a theory to account for it, but his notes showed only a final lack of an explanation. It might be a key fact, but it was one that he had never been able to use.

Harry was sure that it was a case of positive feedback. The mind *knew* it was going insane, so it feared; the helpless fear led to insanity, and the insanity fed the fear! The brain was overloaded and went into oscillation, like an electronic oscillator with its output returned to its input. And like all uncontrolled positive feedback, the process was extremely fast. Of course, if there were some way to apply a negative feedback to balance it . . .

He had been over that hopeless problem too often. Now he shrugged it aside. His mind was still somewhat disturbed by the brief flash that it had received, but he forced it toward the more immediate needs that confronted him.

He had tried a mixture of drugs, hoping that the combination would insure a wild response. In that, he had failed. This time it might be better to concentrate on a larger dose of a single drug. Since LSD seemed to have the worst record for producing bad trips, it would be the logical choice—if there could be any logic to the whole business.

There were other factors that might work for him, too. He was only partially recovered from his first experience, and his tolerance to any bad effects might be reduced. Additionally, the vague depression he still felt could serve to stimulate darker responses; at least in the case of alcohol, the attitude of the user had an effect on the mood induced.

He found the drugs where he had left them and selected what he hoped was the right dose. According to what he'd read, it was barely within normal limits. He took it in the bathroom, washing it down with water from a glass that tasted faintly of toothpaste. Then he moved back to the chair, to sit staring at the clock.

Ellen came in quietly, drying her hands on a towel. She made no protest this time, but went woodenly to the chair facing him and sank onto it. Her knuckles were white as she twisted the towel over them. Her face was blank, but her eyes seemed to be dark pits under the harsh light from overhead.

He tried to reach her mind, but it was cut off from him by a shield under tighter control than he had realized she could manage.

"I'm not going. I couldn't go to bed and leave you like this," she told him flatly. Surprisingly, she'd been able to read his intent, even through the rigidly held impenetrability of her own thoughts. "Oh, Harry!"

It was a hopeless, forlorn cry. And with it, her mind seemed to open for a split second, to send one compressed message of love and unity with him. Then her shield was tight again, blanking out her thoughts. There had been something behind her message that he had almost caught and that now nagged at him. He debated forcing his way past her resistance. But the idea was repugnant to him; besides, he was in no condition to try a test of powers now.

There was no alteration in the ticking of the clock this time, nor any apparent change in the rate at which the hands moved. He let his head sink back, staring through half-closed eyes at Ellen and the clock behind her, curiously free from either fear or anticipation.

The clock surrounded her slowly, without disturbing her. She was now only a heart among its petals, with the minute hand moving across her in a soft, slithering caress. He stared down from his height at her, bringing her closer to him each time she seemed to fade into the distance. It grew harder as she seemed intent on escaping into her clock creche. He frowned, forcing her back.

He floated gently now, weaving slightly with the effort of controlling the pendulum-swing of the Ellen-clock toward him and away again. Then his control increased, and he held the distance firmly, squirm as she would to get away from his power.

He reached for her mind, and her resistance was only a weak thing as the might of his power touched her. Her shield blew away in an inky cloud of little drops that spread outward. They seemed to soak up some of the light. The distant walls of the room were dimmer now, with dark splotches where the shield drops had struck.

Out of the corner of his eye, he saw one of the drops begin to move. He swung about from his height, but the movement stopped before he could fix it with his gaze. Now another drop began to wriggle free from the darkness of its tunnel in the wall.

He hung quietly, letting his sight spread outward. Little by little, his vision broadened until he could see everything around him. Now he could even see the chair in which he had sat. There was a face staring up now——his own face, but younger and filled with an odd fear. Other faces were moving from the tunnels in the walls, and the three new ones were clock-encysted, like the staring white face of Ellen. There were lines between the four faces, dark lines of red that patterned them into a mandala that turned slowly about under him, weaving the lines, spinning and shrouding!

He willed them away. They went slowly, still spinning. And now they were a trap of darkness that began blotting up the light in the great space around him, drawing it into the brown and red funnel that twirled and sucked below him.

He rose above the trap, struggling with a resistance that sucked and climbed after him. But his powers were still too great. He broke free from the trap, rising endlessly into the void above him, until it was all around him. And as he broke free, he realized that it had all been a trick against

166

him. The trap had never been for him, but rather for the light. Now it had been sucked away from him, and he floated in total darkness, unrelieved by stars or planets. There was no light, and his temptation to use his powers had led him beyond the universe, into the great darkness where no god had ever gone.

He reached outward with his mind, thrusting past infinity. But it was hopeless. The void fled with his reach, its limits moving as fast as his mind.

He was no longer floating effortlessly. He was falling. His body flashed downward, accelerating savagely to some fantastic pull. He could feel the void burning his face from the speed of his fall. Somewhere below him, blacker shapes of darkness sucked him downward, opening and closing, then opening again in anticipation of his fall.

He drew in his breath for a desperate effort, but there was no air to breathe! Around him was only foul vacuum. The moisture of his eyes and the saliva of his mouth evaporated out into it in streams of dark-shrouded steam. Little things came to pursue the steam trails, following them down toward his eyes, while his chest slowly collapsed and his body drew upward through his gullet.

And below him, blacker than the dark of the void, lay the Alien Entity, reaching for him with its sucking dendrite arms, slavering as it tasted . . .

From somewhere, a scream reached him!

The darkness vanished, leaving him awash in a dull gray cloud. Somewhere in his mind, he groped and strove toward the scream. But the grayness drew tighter against him, wrapping him about in layers of something that lacked all feeling except squeezing tightness.

He gave up then. It was his own fault. He had sinned. His soul was as tainted as his body, tainted beyond humanity or godhood. Fire had touched him and failed to cleanse him. His taint was too deep, too all-pervading . . .

Something wailed and gibbered!

The grayness was gone, and he sat in a chair in a room of pallid light and narrow walls. His eyes focused on an empty chair and a clock with frozen hands. His vision was a tunnel ahead of him, and he could not lift or turn.

Something moved at his feet, but he could not look down. Something breathed harshly.

Something screamed again, both in his mind and in his ears!

"Ellen!"

The cry was a burst of pain from his throat. From somewhere inside himself, he drew an unknown reserve of strength, enough to tear his eyes from the clock and force his neck to move. Hell beyond reckoning laced through him, but his muscles obeyed his will.

Ellen lay on the floor, her legs twisted under her and her face turned sideways toward him. Her mouth was distorted into a taut grimace of fear, and her eyes were frozen open. Her hands were claws that dug at the rug, with blood oozing from the skin where her efforts had abraided it.

There was no shield over her mind now. Her thoughts screamed toward him, the horror and fear in them piercing through the muddle of drugs and memory in his brain.

The strain of watching over his fantasy-horrors had been the final stress beyond her limit. Now her vision of madness was fulfilled. And the real horror was that a tiny spark of the real Ellen knew her madness and desperately reached to him for help.

He started toward her. The room seemed to swell and spin around him. He was moving again through illusion.

## XV.

## DELAY

The driveway of the so-called rest home was in darkness as Dr. Philip Lawson guided his big car away from the gate, but there were lights showing in some of the windows. He pulled into a parking space near the main building and turned toward the old figure on the seat beside him.

"Were you ever here before, Charley?"

Grimes put down the papers he had been studying in forlorn hope and shook his head curtly. "No, I depend on regular reports. She couldn't stand me, Phil. I was the Grim Man to her, even before what happened. But I had to have it like this for her. She could never have stood the cure you went through."

Lawson left him behind and headed across the rich turf and up the walk to the main entrance. There was a woman at the desk whom he'd never met, but he was expected this time. Dr. MacAndrews was waiting for him in the private room toward which she directed him. The man was yawning over a cup of coffee and a clipboard of papers. He waved aside Lawson's apologies for getting him up and held out the papers.

Strange how that gesture conveyed the respect of one honest physician for another! It had been a long time since Lawson had found anything but contempt from those who had once been his peers, though the imaginary ills he

169

treated had roots deeper than the tumors they could reach. But at least MacAndrews could understand, if not wholly approve.

There was nothing in the records of Martha Bronson that had not been covered in the report Grimes had received. Her long wait was nearly finished. There was a clearly inoperable growth in her brain, already threatening certain vital areas. But she was somewhat more rational now during the periods when she was permitted to regain consciousness.

He knew now that his last trip here to threaten her with terrors keyed to her fantasies had been almost pointless; even without his intervention, she could have found few chances to invade the mind of her son. And perhaps it hadn't mattered, after all.

"Can I see her now, Mac?" he asked.

MacAndrews nodded reluctantly. "I suppose so, Phil. But she's under heavy sedation. I can bring her out, but . . ."

Lawson checked the papers again for the drug being used, then tapped the bag he had brought. "No problem. I've got something here that will leave her under full analgesia."

MacAndrews started to protest, then shrugged tiredly. He led the way through the corridors and to the long hall at the rear. Abruptly, he stopped and turned to confront Lawson.

"How much do you remember?" he asked.

"Enough to know what it felt like—how good it was at first," Lawson answered. "Nothing more. And you?"

MacAndrews seemed to strain for something momentarily. Then his face sagged again. "Not even that. I guess I waited too long. If it weren't for you and hints I get from your wife, I'd believe it was all just part of my fantasizing. Oh, hell!"

"You're better off that way," Lawson assured him. It was the bitter truth, as a thousand nights of useless straining had taught him, before his quest for odd drugs had given him some outlet for his needs.

MacAndrews nodded vaguely and seemed to dismiss the

170

subject. He lifted a small covering over a spyhole and glanced through it out of habit. Then he opened the door with his key and motioned Lawson through, taking up a post just outside.

Martha was lying in drugged sleep, her bloated body limp under the sheet. The soft illumination of the room was kind to her, but it could not wholly conceal the ugly ravages of time.

He stared at her with no particular emotion. She had been his wife once, one who should have been closer than any normal human could conceive. But there had never been any real closeness; she had kept her chilled thoughts to herself, denying him her mind as carefully as she had wanted to deny him his other rights.

He bent over her now, slipping the sheet back to inject the exotic drug that would best serve his purpose. Finished, he sat on the foot of the bed to wait for her response.

All the love of which she was capable had gone to her only son. It had been a possessive love, at that. And Philip Bronson had let the boy mean everything to him, too. Young Harry had been a prodigy, far beyond what could be expected. A link had been established between them, almost as soon as the boy could talk. There seemed to be little clairvoyant power in the young mind—perhaps because the changes in the growing personality came too quickly for easy attunement to the future—but the telepathic ability had been phenomenal. Bronson had dared to hope that the strength and talent of his son were enough to overcome what Coleman had begun to think was the usual fate of their kind.

Then had come Martha's betrayal of the child in the horror of her attempted immolation, while he was so sunk in the despair of his own foreknown doom that he had nearly failed to realize what she must intend. His return had been too late to save the boy from the shock of being in her mind during that horror—almost too late to save them physically.

Looking back, Lawson still could not estimate how sane his actions had been then. But within the limits of his tottering reason, he had fought honestly to find a way to save the tortured mind of his son. His first efforts had failed, overcome by the lingering connection that still existed between the boy and Martha. In the end, he'd been forced to block both memory and talent from the young mind, barely succeeding within the time he had. It was only on the last day during which he could trust himself that he had given Harry to Charley Grimes with instructions that should preserve his work. And later, after the grim but dim years of recovery, he had been forced to accept Grimes' decision to keep the boy.

His hope had been that the suppressed talents would eventually reappear, gradually attaining their full force in a mind grown old and mature enough to handle them safely. It had been a shock to learn that the abilities remained buried. He hadn't believed Coleman's reports until he'd managed to gain entry to the Primates and study his son for himself.

Lawson sighed, seeing the first change in Martha's breathing as the drug took effect. How often must a man robbed of all his powers continue to play god? How many mistakes could he make?

Could a surgeon let his son go through life without vision because of cataracts that could be removed? The answer had seemed simple, despite the risks, when he had used trickery and hypnotism to remove the blocks he had so carefully built. But now . . .

Would that drug never work on this wreck of a woman?

There were all the notes Harry had made to be read after Grimes had the apartment opened in hopes of finding clues to their current location. Harry had always kept copious notes of his thoughts when doing schoolwork, and the habit had remained. They had revealed nothing of any destination. But they had revealed too much else, though nothing that was clear. Insanity, possession, something about an Alien Entity . . .

Drat Hillery and his stupid games. And a double pox on the detective who had let the kids slip out of his watch! Maybe there was nothing that could be done for Harry and Ellen. But he had to try. He had to be there!

Martha stirred at last. She opened her eyes and stared up

172

at him, muttering thickly, lifting one hand in an ancient sign to ward off evil. He bent closer, trying to catch the words. She was making little sense—something about the Man in White, her symbol for him. He spoke soothingly, calling her name, trying to reassure her.

Once he could have known surely what he needed. But now he was blind and halt, and he must depend on even such a festering remnant as this. She might still be able to tell him—if she would.

She caught her breath, and her expression cleared. This time she seemed to feel none of the fear she had screamed at him during their last encounter.

"I'm dead," she said quietly.

"I know, Martha," he agreed. He'd decoded some of the fantasies behind her ravings long since. "But they can't let you go yet. Not until they can find the Boy. He must be cleaned of sin, too. You know that, don't you, Martha?"

She nodded heavily. He'd expected a long session, but she seemed exhausted and almost glad to give in to the right appeal. "He's over the river and through the trees," said slowly. "I can't say more. You'll know. If you're not one of them, you'll know."

The river must be the Hudson—there weren't many trees in the other direction. That meant New Jersey. And there were two possible places there, if he remembered what Grimes had told him. It had to be one of them.

He opened the door and nodded at MacAndrews. But Martha suddenly giggled shrilly.

"Too late," she cried. "The Man in White is too late. Always too late! Too late!"

## XVI.

## RETURN

Harry saw the living room couch ahead of him, thickly shrouded with crying shadows. He bent toward it, guarding the weight in his arms from the ropy ooze of the ceiling. The couch retreated as he advanced, seeming to melt at one end and flow to the other.

He blanked his mind to the screaming that seemed to be coming from his arms and reached far back into his memories, groping across hard gulfs toward something he had known. Then he saw it; from the doorway to the couch was only about eight steps. He took one step, then another, counting carefully. The couch still retreated, but something touched his leg at the eighth step. He hardened his mind and looked again. This time, the couch was in front of him, wriggling about but not moving away.

He put the thing he carried down carefully, to see that it had been Ellen's body. Her face was twisted, and her arms were threshing wildly, while his own arms felt sore and had red streaks down them. Was that more fantasy, or was it real? He focused his eyes with care and decided that the streaks were real gashes in his skin from her nails and that she really was acting strangely.

The reality came back to him in a sick flash of sureness.

174

This was no hallucination. Ellen had gone mad, and he had found her writhing on the floor. He had picked her up to take her to the bedroom, but had somehow turned the wrong way. It didn't matter, he decided; the couch here would serve, since it seemed to be quiet now.

He sent out a probe toward her. His mind touched a foulness that he had once known from precognition, but the horror that had been foreshadowed for him was only a faint image of this reality.

Her thoughts boiled at his touch, begging for help and shrieking in fear of him. He heard her scream, felt his own throat contract in a harsh gargling sound, and then his mind ripped itself free from her. It was too much; no sane mind could force itself to plumb the depths of such horror.

Pithecanthropus slunk through her thoughts, lusting his animal evil and fearing his unknowably gruesome demons. Neanderthaler screamed in superstitious dread as the night fell on him, while his wily mind considered dark things to follow his cannibal feast. Civilized Caligula watched the murder of his kinsmen, trembling but drooling for the throne and the godhood that carried his death.

Below that lay depths without images or consciousness, reaching back into the slime of primordial retchings.

Harry wanted to be sick, but his stomach was too taut with shock to convulse.

This was no paranoia as he had read of it, no schizophrenia he had discovered. It was the basic source of all madness, too dark for name or description. Yet its horror stemmed from the consciousness that still operated within her, crying to him and to herself, touching still the person she had been. Somewhere, the Ellen he loved was mixed into everything else in her mind, and she knew . . .

Great God, how well she knew!

He dropped beside her, his muscles crawling at the contact with the vessel into which such filth could be poured. Yet he raised one arm and put it around her, hoping that the Ellen-self could feel it and know its message, however much it might also frighten and assault her other reactions. He could only hope; he could not force himself to enter that mind again to know.

From the shadows of the room, just beyond the edge of his vision, shapes began to slither out. The walls were moving inward, bringing *something* with them . . .

He felt the taste of blood in his mouth as he bit down to control himself. Sweat trickled into his eyes, and he writhed and moaned as he fought. Then the walls were back and normal, and the shapes were gone. He lay panting, straining to hold onto himself.

He was sure she must have had warning. The brief flash of madness he had felt while preparing himself for his second trip must have been from her mind. That was why she had kept him away from her thoughts and why she had gathered her shield around the knot of her mind. She had realized it was coming, had already felt its first touches. And still she had bent to his will and had tried to control herself to watch over him during his playing at madness with the drugs. She had sat with her fear for him mounting onto her fear for herself and had never used the one claim she had with which to wrench him from his stupid plan! In the end, she had broken. But to the last second, she had fought her battle alone, rather than impose her demands on him!

Now, when she needed him as no woman had ever needed a man, he was a distorted shell of himself, slackly given over to the control of a chemical that could supply weakling gods to frightened atheists, but which could never provide truth or strength to deal with reality.

He felt that the drug had not yet begun to weaken, but he could not afford to wait for it to abate, or still longer while he could regain his control. Every second that passed for him was an eon of destruction within her mind. Yet he knew of no antidote or means of ending the hold of the drug on him.

He pressed himself desperately against Ellen, reaching into his own now-treacherous mind for what he had no other way of finding. He had felt the mind of others who used drugs and had read all that he could find on the subject. But there was no answer in his memories. He had to trust whatever passed for intuition within him, knowing that it was probably untrustworthy now.

Men could pull themselves free of the influence of alcohol under extreme stress—at least for a brief time. Even the supposedly incurably insane sometimes could meet emergencies with short periods of rational thought. Harry vaguely remembered something about men in mid-trip who could force themselves back to normality when they chose. But no sense of how it was done seemed to have been provided by them.

He had taken the first step, however. He had recognized that his mind was subject to hallucinations already and had forced himself to deny their control over him. But could he maintain his awareness while he tried to turn his mind to whatever else he must do?

He fought within himself to force his mind above any level that could be affected by the drug he had taken. He stared at the walls, seeing them still solid and normal. There were dark skitterings at the edge of his consciousness, but they seemed to creep back into nothingness as he worked on them. For the moment he felt wholly himself—but a weakened self, one horribly unsure of how long he could maintain his control.

He could not think consciously of what he must do. He should be planning his steps in detail, but he knew he dared not think of even the initial move; conscious attention to what he must face would numb his will and send him into shivering fits.

Coffee! His body sent up a cry for it, while he knew that it could probably do no good. The demand was only an attempt to put off action for a few moments more. Yet habit insisted he fortify himself with the stimulant before any effort could begin.

He tore himself away from the couch and headed for the kitchen, forcing himself to hold the floor steady before his eyes. He found the pot half full and poured the cold fluid into a cup. He downed it without cream or sugar, then poured another and swallowed it hastily. And finally, hating every step, he turned back to the living room and the writhing figure of Ellen on the couch. He used his belt to fasten her hands clumsily, shoved her toward the wall, and sank beside her.

His mind plunged into hers. The dampers on her emotions were gone, leaving no control over the wild overreaction of positive feedback. His first touch became a demon invasion, a wanton orgy of rape and torture, a terror beyond tolerance.

Reluctantly, he opened his own perceptions, searching for what he must do. The ugliness and all the fears and angers of a lifetime, the rages and hatreds, spread through him. All his unknown hopes were hopeless now, he saw. There was no way to find any rationality to use within her against the unreason of her madness. No mental suasion would suffice. What passed for thoughts within her brain could no longer respond or be bent to the normal ways. Only a drastic psychic surgery and excision could offer her salvation.

The distortion of her mind began fighting him. He had never appreciated before how strong that mind was. Now he felt the full power of her desperation turned against his intrusion. Her mind seemed to claw its way down to the bedrock of her animal cells and there stand fast to repel him. He could not operate within it, could not absorb what lay around his awareness. She thrust him out.

He must have been screaming, since his throat was a raging sore and his lungs were gasping for breath in a harsh rasping. He had taken too much. He could never perform the acts he must do.

It had to be done. But ethically, morally, humanly—it was impossible. No man could treat a living mind in such a way. Only a subhuman sadist would deliberately disfigure even the body of another person.

No! The highest ethics and sensitivity of his surgeon father had demanded that he cut relentlessly until the last trace of malignancy was removed. Yet without anesthesia . . . patient's consent . . . trained skill and knowledge . . . But who had greater skill in this?

Every value and absolute within him was in turmoil, deadlocked in a private Armageddon. Right was wrong, and wrong was right. He felt his mind lurch and shift . . .

And something moved into his awareness. It was a thing

178

of distorted values, ruthless strangeness—alien! It was his Alien Entity, claiming him now when his mind was divided and he had no will to waste in fighting it.

He held onto himself, determined not to be thrust aside again. But there was no counterthrust of pressure, no attempt to force him out of control. This was the most subtle of invasions. The alien values slipped among his contending judgments, making links where no connections should be. The presence was muting the full force he had felt once before, and it was becoming less alien to him—or he to it. All he could feel surely was the power within it, a determined might that his own mind found wanting within itself. It could take him, use him, own him . . .

Ellen moaned, and he looked down at her again. He shuddered, feeling the persuasion of the determination, the alien sureness of the mind within his mind. Then he sighed. Nothing really mattered now except his desperate need to save Ellen. To that end, no price was too great. Let her find salvation and he would accept the evil thereof!

He screamed a silent bargain toward his Alien Entity and opened himself in full acceptance.

There was no longer war within him. He was a narrow self, driven into a single purpose. He no longer had a name or a body; he could feel and know nothing but the darkness he must meet and the purpose he must achieve.

There was still opposition to his entry into Ellen's mind, but it began to fail almost at once before the drive of his determination. His mind tightened ruthlessly, driving her back, until there were no barriers to his invasion.

He found the depths of horror and took them for his own. Her childish, forsaken aloneness became his, and his mind wailed and gibbered with abandonment, with desertion, with its total outcast state. He took each pain until he throbbed with agony. He swallowed the angers until rage burned like a nova in him. He found the hatred and all the foul poisons bestowed by a thousand generations, and he made a feast of them for his memories.

From some unthinking distance, a disturbance reached him faintly, distracting him briefly. There was a sound of

179

pounding. A wind blew across him, chilling his sweating body, and things seemed to claw at him, trying to tear him away. He tightened his arms and thrust aside exterior perception or illusion.

He had no word for the thing that must be done. The symbols for such nouns and verbs did not exist. But the force within him now did not falter as it broke and twisted synaptic links, burned memory banks, and began altering and restructuring the mind that had been all he had ever dared love fully. Nothing was now alien to the alien mind he had become. Had precognition warned him fully of this, he would have escaped willingly into madness. But he went on now, coldly, relentlessly, until the work was done.

Then his consciousness of self slipped out of his grasp. His ego was gone, and he blanked out into a writhing void of chaos within himself.

Awareness returned slowly, with a sense that much time had passed. He held his consciousness to a low, dim level. But there was light against his eyes, forcing him to open them. He saw that it came from a raised window, through which a gentle breeze was blowing. It was cool against his skin, and there was a scent of growing things.

Behind him, there was the sound of someone stirring. He started to turn, feeling his muscles ache with soreness. A hand touched his forehead.

"It's eleven o'clock, son—in the forenoon. You've been asleep for ten hours," a voice said quietly. "How do you feel?"

He stretched slowly, groaning as he did so. His body ached at every joint, but the worst pain seemed to center on his diaphragm. He saw that he was lying on a couch in Greenwald's living room. A man was sitting in a chair beside him, and he recognized the tired face as that of Dr. Philip Lawson.

"I don't know, yet," he answered honestly. His throat was sore, and his voice sounded hoarse; but for some reason, his physical condition didn't seem to matter. He started to consider his mental state, but there was a veil

180

across his thoughts, and he felt an uneasy reluctance to look behind it.

"Feel up to walking out to the kitchen?"

He nodded. His legs felt stiff but gained in sureness as he began to use them. He took the chair Lawson drew out for him, then looked up quickly as Grimes placed a steaming cup of coffee before him.

"You'll feel better with some of this under your belt, Henry," the lawyer said, his old face twisted into something like a smile. "I made it myself."

It tasted that way, but it was strong and hot. Harry swallowed it with a nod of thanks. "What's going on?"

"Read the answer for yourself," Lawson suggested, gesturing toward his forehead. There was a drawn look on his face. Grimes stiffened, then quickly moved back to the stove where he was making a pot of tea.

Harry stretched out his mind, reaching only for surface thoughts, as he'd learned to do with those lacking mutant powers. But Lawson had once been a mutant; his mind was open, with an amazingly well-organized picture of events.

"You can still read me?" The thought was low but intense.

Harry nodded assent. He was surprised to remember that there should have been a loss of ability from the strain he had undergone. The surface facts stood out clearly, ending with the two men rushing through the night and breaking into the house to find him as rigid as a statue with Ellen clutched in his arms.

"Ellen?" he asked sharply.

Lawson's hand pressed him back to the chair. "Easy, son. She's sleeping now, under sedation, and I don't think we should disturb her. When she regained consciousness, she seemed a little afraid of you, so we had to move her to the bedroom. She acted confused, though her responses were fairly rational. I think she'll be all right."

"She's a child again!" Grimes protested.

Lawson smiled slightly at the lawyer, assuming his professional manner. "Naturally. Normal reaction to deep psychological trauma, Charley. She should recover with time and rest. Anyhow, Harry could help her."

Grimes frowned, but did not argue. He picked up his cup of tea and left them, heading for the bedroom to watch over Ellen.

A child! Harry considered it uncertainly. That might mean she was the child she would have been if the madness of her parents had never happened and if all the ugliness had remained undiscovered. Or it might mean so much of her was missing that she could never be more. He could determine which—but his mind refused to probe, somehow sure that he must wait.

Lawson sat quietly as Harry poured two more cups of the muddy coffee for them. He spooned out sugar carefully, staring at the cup. Then he shrugged and raised his eyes, while every line in his face deepened.

"Harry could help her," he repeated. "He would. But will you? Last night I gave you a special sedative. Oh, you needed it, but I needed its side effects more, after reading all those notes you left behind. I needed to learn whether you were my son, a madman, or an alien monster. I still don't know. The drug didn't work on you."

He lifted his eyes again, as if driven to meet something he was reluctant to find.

"Harry, who are you?"

The veil that had lain across Harry's mind dropped, letting him remember everything. The reality of what he was flooded through him. It was too much to grasp at once, but he accepted it, adjusted to it, and became it. Some of it was what he had grown into over many years, and some was only unfulfilled growth-promise. It was a hopelessly tangled web of shifting values, ever in flux, but always himself.

He scanned it in a single burst of comprehension. Then he began moving out, closing himself down, saving himself for later thought and adjustment. Deliberately this time, he regressed until he was no more than his father could accept or than his previous social patterns could handle.

He met Lawson's anxious eyes and managed a familiar smile. "No philosopher ever found the answer to that ques-

182

tion. But I'm Harry Bronson—reasonably sane, with no outside monster in my head."

"You're trying to convince me that every fact of precognition can be wrong? Harry, it won't wash. I remember enough to know better!"

"No. Every *fact* was correct." Harry smiled again. "Only the interpretation was wrong. But didn't you once tell me that false interpretation of true symptoms was the greatest risk in medicine?"

Now some of the tension left Lawson's face. He sat back in his chair, beginning to relax as he reached for a pipe and tobacco. "In everything, son. Men can check their data, and they usually manage to agree pretty well on the facts. But they keep filling battlegrounds, prisons, asylums, and cemeteries because of the interpretations they make. Yes, I'll buy that. Misinterpretation is the most deadly of human sins. Umm. What about the madness?"

"The shock and terror of that were real—but it was Ellen's madness, with my mind so completely linked to hers that I couldn't tell the difference. I should have guessed, however; no two human minds could go mad in exactly the same way, as we seemed to do."

"And your demon—the Alien Entity you experienced?"

Harry grimaced wryly, remembering his horror but no longer able to understand it. He should have guessed that, too; his pondering on maturity and his changes during childhood through regression should have given him the answer. "That was real—and alien, I suppose. But it was no monster from outside myself. It was only the foreshadowing of what is—or will be—myself."

He sighed, seeing the lack of understanding in Lawson's mind. In his present, closed-down state, it was something he also found difficult to understand fully. But he tried to shape his thoughts and explain in ways the other man could accept.

To a child, living in an eternal now of desire and outside restraints, nothing could be more alien than the values and behavior of adults. Why should a man do a lot of hard things he didn't like just to keep some girl happy, or let her run his life when he was stronger than she was? Why should he risk war, work, and traffic—and then be scared to climb a simple old tree on a dare? Why wouldn't he eat green apples when he drank stuff that tasted bad and always made him sick? Why put money in somebody else's bank when he wanted a lot of things he could buy with it?

The adolescent knew about responsibility—the responsibility of the alien-minded men running things, who must be evil since they refused the simple, obvious answers. But he couldn't understand why those adults laughed at him for driving thousands of miles in a car to help bury a broken auto engine and thus end pollution symbolically. The move from the certainties of adolescence to the complexity of adulthood was so difficult that many retreated to schizophrenia or acquired authority-figures who would take over the responsibilities they could not assume. Maybe a majority eventually learned to live with reality, but only a minority could accept the fact that even reality was neither fixed nor sure. Yet they had grown up in a world where a thousand generations had built an adult tradition and where every effort had been made to instill the desire for adulthood into their minds since infancy.

There had been no examples to guide Harry's development, no body of adult mutant values to be studied and gradually accepted. He had never realized his lack of adulthood—since he was already a full adult by the standards of nonmutant society.

Effectively, he had been a child, forced to face his mature self from the future. And the horror had not lain in the wrongness he saw in its values, but in the fact that it was himself—a self he could not accept and had to hide from his own awareness.

"So there never was any real danger for you?" Lawson asked doubtfully. Then he shook his head. "No, that's unfair. Living through an accident doesn't prove there was no danger. But with precognition?"

"Precognition doesn't settle the old problem of free will, any more than the normal rules of cause and effect," Harry told him. He could not explain away the seeming paradox, but he knew it was true. "The danger was real—too real!"

184

The price of the gift was the gift itself, together with the good and the evil thereof. It was an ancient price, changed only in degree. Man had gained intelligence beyond any other animal. But his sufferings and burdens were as unique as his advantages and pleasures. The price of any increase in awareness was inherent in that awareness.

It was little wonder the others had gone mad. The stresses of extrasensory sensitivity could only be handled by a new maturity—and that maturity was alien and horrible to all they had been taught. There was no acceptable answer to the problem. Both problem and answer fed back positively to increase stress and insure sudden, foreknown madness!

He had barely survived, mostly by luck. The amnesiac block had let him cope with the normal adjustment to adulthood before the new problem had to be met, rather than facing both demands together. Even the drugs had helped, though his reasons for seeking them had been wrong; they had disturbed his fixed patterns enough to weaken his resistance to other ways of thought. Even then, his own needs could not have made him accept maturity; it had been the necesssity of helping Ellen that had finally forced him to grow up.

"I was lucky," he decided aloud.

"No, not lucky. Strong!" There was satisfaction in Lawson's smile and a deep glow of pride in his mind. "We always thought you were the strongest one of us all, and we were right. Admit your strength, son, and be glad of it. We need you. We've waited a long time for you to lead us into our future!"

Harry started to protest. Then he saw the hidden hunger in his father's mind and made no argument. "All right, maybe you're right, Dad. Unless I've simply postponed my madness and it's still waiting for me later."

"Look ahead and see," Lawson suggested. "What else is precognition good for?"

The test seemed obvious. There would be no true sense of safety until he could be sure. But he hesitated, unwilling to risk it. For the moment, there was no dark cloud over his mind, and the sensation of relief was precious. He turned

Lawson's words over, considering. Maybe it wasn't precognition that had survival value, after all; it might be something he could only term postcognition—the ability to reach backward to assist, as his future self must have helped him in handling the twisted mind of Ziggy. Maybe . . .

The future opened calmly to him. It came like a memory, with a partial sense of what had gone before and with sound and vision as clear as if he had been living through it. Yet there was no sense of identity in the sending; somehow, he was gently blocked from the thoughts of his future self.

Lawson grunted sharply, then caught his breath in a harsh gasp of emotion. And Harry was aware that his vision was being shared by his father. Subtle but enormous power was being used, opening the old channels of lost abilities for the moment. Then his own awareness sank fully into his precognition.

Winter was over again, and the ice was gone; but the little creek was still too cold for swimming or wading. He lay on the young grass, sheltered from the fresh wind that was blowing beyond him. Across the little bridge lay an old stone house, mellow with years and associations. His eyes swept over it and across the enclosed grounds.

A babble of childish speech reached his ears then, and he turned to look further down the creek toward a tiny beach. His three-year-old son was standing there, one foot held over the water and the other on the sand. The boy was facing his grandfather, trying to determine from the thoughts in Lawson's mind whether the threat of punishment had been serious. He reached forward with his foot, then splashed in happily, while Lawson ran toward him, swearing but laughing.

Harry felt a slight surge within himself. Then the childish babble was cut off. Reluctantly but steadily, the boy's feet headed out of the chilly water and toward the shoes he had discarded. Harry settled back in the warm sun, gazing across the sweep of his acres. It was a restful place, a place to which a man might return in triumph or to seek relief from fatigue, a haven and a home.

There was a sense of opening outward—and the presence was there. Again it came with the feeling of immeasurable distance and gulfs beyond imagination. It came on its never-ending lonely search, reaching softly toward him. It was totally alien, yet warm with friendliness beyond that which humanity had learned.

For a second, it seemed to sweep past him. Then it was back, intense and aware with a sudden knowledge that he was there.

There was no communication. No bridges existed yet to span the difference of thought or provide a key for conceptual exchange. There was only a meeting and entwining.

The presence lingered for a moment, somehow conveying a sense that it would soon return. There was something that might have been the exultant praise of a father to a clever child before the presence was gone.

Harry's precognition faded, leaving only a faint memory of that benison. He stared at his father, noticing that there were tears in Lawson's eyes. Then full realization hit him, and he leaped to his feet, shoving the chair back.

"Ellen!" There had been no sign of her in his vision, though the child might have been hers.

But there was no unusual worry on Grimes' face as the lawyer looked up at their entrance.

Ellen lay on the bed. Her face was that of a sleeping child. Her lips were swollen from the wounds that she had inflicted on herself, and her torn fingers lay swathed in bandages. She had been washed, and her hair was combed back. There was no tension anywhere in her.

Harry probed very gently at her thoughts. The hell through which she had gone and the brutal means of her return could have burned away her powers, just as shock treatments had destroyed those of Lawson. Her mind was quiet now, filled with sleep rhythms that seemed natural. Then there was awareness of him, a welcome that needed no words, and she turned toward him. If she had feared him before, that fear was gone.

Her response seemed less rich and greatly weakened. But strength could be developed again, so long as her talents were not wholly gone. He probed further carefully, finding scars and areas that were closed down, as if too sore to be used. But she was at peace within herself now.

Then her eyes opened, and she sat up, staring at them for a moment. She nodded and smiled at them, the little girl smile she had worn in her sleep. But the feel of her mind in Harry's was stronger now, and she seemed to draw strength from him.

"Hello, Harry," she said. "I'm tired of this place. I want to go back to our home."

Harry nodded and smiled down at her, while Grimes beamed his approval.

"All right, honey," Harry told her. "We'll go back. We're done here and we'll go home as soon as I can pack."

The interlude was over.

# XVII.

## AMEN

Professor Harris looked down at the large gray rat in the cage before him, nodding impatiently at the nervous explanations pouring from the mouth of young Jones. The rat stared back calmly, neither seeking nor avoiding his eyes.

"He just wouldn't go crazy," Jones was repeating. "We tried everything. Jenny—Miss Simpson, I mean—she thought we must have done something wrong. So we put him in with the second batch and ran it all over again. But he wouldn't react! You can see the others over in the big cage. They all went into shock. But he—"

Harris nodded again, trying to pretend interest. He'd read the report already. They had tried every type of pressure and unexpected punishment on the rat they called Muley. They confused rewards and punishments, mixed food with electric shocks, and generally made life hell for the poor little beast. But Muley refused to cooperate; he simply accepted the whim of fate and waited them out.

Now Harris cut off the flow of words. "All right, Jones. You'd better dispose of those others."

"And Muley?"

"Muley?" Harris smiled down at the rat, then began

189

opening the cage. "No, Jones. Nothing that simple for him. I've been waiting twenty years to find one of his kind. I've got a lot of special things for him."

He picked up the rat in his hands and went out, stroking the gray fur approvingly. Muley stared back at him calmly.

12-72